Check into the Pennyfoot Hotel . . .
for delightful tales of detection!

Room with a Clue

The view from the Pennyfoot's roof garden is lovely—
but for Lady Eleanor Danbury, it was the last thing
she ever saw. Now Cecily must find out who sent the
snobbish society matron falling to her death . . .

Do Not Disturb

Mr. Bickley answered the door knocker and ended up
dead. Cecily must capture the culprit—before murder
darkens another doorstep . . .

Service for Two

Dr. McDuff's funeral became a fiasco when the
mourners found a stranger's body in the casket. Now
Cecily must close the case—for at the Pennyfoot,
murder is a most unwelcome guest . . .

MORE MYSTERIES FROM THE
BERKLEY PUBLISHING GROUP . . .

THE INSPECTOR AND MRS. JEFFRIES: He's with Scotland Yard. She's his housekeeper. Sometimes, her job can be murder . . .

by Emily Brightwell

THE INSPECTOR AND MRS. JEFFRIES
MRS. JEFFRIES DUSTS FOR CLUES

THE GHOST AND MRS. JEFFRIES
MRS. JEFFRIES TAKES STOCK

JENNY McKAY MYSTERIES: This TV reporter finds out where, when, why . . . *and* whodunit. "A more streetwise version of television's 'Murphy Brown.'" —*Booklist*

by Dick Belsky

BROADCAST CLUES
THE MOURNING SHOW

LIVE FROM NEW YORK

CAT CALIBAN MYSTERIES: She was married for thirty-eight years. Raised three kids. Compared to that, tracking down killers is easy . . .

by D. B. Borton

ONE FOR THE MONEY
THREE IS A CROWD

TWO POINTS FOR MURDER

KATE JASPER MYSTERIES: Even in sunny California, there are cold-blooded killers . . . "This series is a treasure!" — Carolyn G. Hart

by Jaqueline Girdner

ADJUSTED TO DEATH
THE LAST RESORT
TEA-TOTALLY DEAD

MURDER MOST MELLOW
FAT-FREE AND FATAL

RENAISSANCE MYSTERIES: Sigismondo the sleuth courts danger—and sheds light on the darkest of deeds . . . "Most entertaining!" — *Chicago Tribune*

by Elizabeth Eyre

DEATH OF THE DUCHESS

PENNYFOOT HOTEL MYSTERIES: In Edwardian England, death takes a seaside holiday . . .

by Kate Kingsbury

ROOM WITH A CLUE
SERVICE FOR TWO

DO NOT DISTURB
EAT, DRINK, AND BE BURIED

CHARLOTTE GRAHAM MYSTERIES: She's an actress with a flair for dramatics—and an eye for detection. "You'll get hooked on Charlotte Graham!" —*Rave Reviews*

by Stefanie Matteson

MURDER AT THE SPA
MURDER AT TEATIME
MURDER ON THE CLIFF

MURDER ON THE SILK ROAD
MURDER AT THE FALLS

DEWEY JAMES MYSTERIES: America's favorite small-town sleuth! "Highly entertaining!" —*Booklist*

by Kate Morgan

DAYS OF CRIME AND ROSES

WANTED: DUDE OR ALIVE

A PENNYFOOT HOTEL MYSTERY

EAT, DRINK, AND BE BURIED

KATE KINGSBURY

BERKLEY PRIME CRIME, NEW YORK

EAT, DRINK, AND BE BURIED

A Berkley Prime Crime Book / published by arrangement with the author

PRINTING HISTORY
Berkley Prime Crime edition / September 1994

All rights reserved.
Copyright © 1994 by Doreen Roberts.
This book may not be reproduced in whole or in part,
by mimeograph or any other means, without permission.
For information address: The Berkley Publishing Group,
200 Madison Avenue, New York, NY 10016.

ISBN: 0-425-14352-X

Berkley Prime Crime Books are published by
The Berkley Publishing Group,
200 Madison Avenue, New York, NY 10016.
The name BERKLEY PRIME CRIME and the BERKLEY PRIME CRIME
design are trademarks belonging to Berkley Publishing Corporation.

PRINTED IN THE UNITED STATES OF AMERICA

10 9 8 7 6 5 4 3 2 1

CHAPTER

❖ 1 ❖

They came in the night, during the spring of 1908, slipping quietly through the trees that skirted Putney Downs. The villagers had no inkling of their presence. Not until after the camp had been firmly established, deep in the woods where few people would dare to challenge them.

The first sign of them came in the early morning, with the smoke curling above the leafy branches of the oak trees to mar the clear blue sky. But very soon the evidence of their existence became more annoying.

The sounds of their passionate music and wild laughter floated on the night winds, disturbing the villagers in their sleep. Those adventurous enough to peek caught glimpses of gaily painted caravans, illuminated by the leaping flames of their fires.

Farmers lost pigs and sheep, housewives lost washing

from the line, and fearful mothers warned their children not to play in the woods.

The gypsies had arrived in Badgers End.

Even the most skeptical would not risk the wrath of the gypsies. Crossing their path could result in a curse, or much worse. Far better to leave them alone, in the hopes that soon they would tire of their new habitat and depart before something terrible happened.

Colonel Fortescue had no such thoughts in his mind that late April evening. He had just enjoyed a snifter or two of very good brandy in the George and Dragon, a nightcap to maintain the mellow glow he'd acquired from the gin he'd consumed with dinner at the Pennyfoot Hotel.

Things had been a trifle disorganized at the George. Dick Scroggins had been forced to put the place up for sale, and soon there would be a new owner. Until then, the place floundered like a Punjabi in quicksand.

The colonel had had to wait twice as long to get his brandy, and he was later than usual leaving the noisy warmth of the pub. The darkness that greeted him as he stepped outside took him by surprise. He didn't like to walk alone in the dark.

Apart from the fact that the night spooked the blazes out of him, his eyesight wasn't what it used to be. All that dashed blinking made his eyes water, and in the dark it was like walking in a thick, impenetrable mist.

There didn't seem to be much he could do about it, however. He would just have to put his best foot forward and pretend he was back in India, leading the regiment on dress parade.

Standing at attention, he fastened the buttons of his Norfolk jacket, then, taking a firm hold of his walking stick, he struck out for the Esplanade. Once there the gaslights would illuminate his way back to the Pennyfoot Hotel.

After a while he began to feel extremely tired. It was difficult to march properly when his foot wavered every time he lifted it off the ground. The familiar gin-induced sensation of mounting steps that weren't there, easy enough to deal with in daylight, became rather frightening in the dark—as if he were stepping off an unseen cliff, only to have the ground come up and hit his foot when he least expected it.

And he could have sworn the Esplanade was closer than this. He seemed to have been tramping for blasted miles. Blinking rapidly, a legacy left from the shell shock he'd sustained in the Tropics, the colonel did his best to penetrate the darkness ahead of him.

Just then, to his profound relief, the moon slid out from behind a cloud, casting a pale glow across the grass.

The colonel blinked again. Grass? How the blue blazes did he manage to find grass? He should have kept to the roadside until he'd reached the Esplanade, which swept majestically along the length of the beach on its way to the Pennyfoot.

He must have wandered into a field. Swaying, he steadied himself with his walking stick. In front of him the grass rolled away in a huge, undulating carpet, rising until it stopped abruptly, a clean edge against the dark, star-dotted sky.

Where the devil—?

He heard the soft swish of water combing the sands far below, steadily, one wave after another, the frothy tumble of the ocean as it broke over the rocks farther down the beach. The breeze cuffed his face, salty and damp.

Blinking, he tried desperately to focus on the wavering edge of the carpet that appeared to be suspended in space. He was on top of the cliffs, somewhere on Putney Downs. *Think, man, think.*

He must have got turned around somewhere. All he had to do was retrace his steps, dashed carefully, of course, and he would eventually end up back at the Esplanade. All being well.

Gripping the walking stick, he prodded the ground around him. The end of it sank into soft grass, and then held. He was at least on safe ground for the moment.

Another sound caught his ear, muffled at first, then becoming more distinct as it overcame the harsh whispers of the ocean. Horse's hooves, pounding the turf as if it were running the Grand National race.

His first thought was relief that he was not alone on this quiet night on the Downs. Then he remembered the gypsies.

Ghastly stories he had heard muttered in the saloon bar at the George and Dragon filtered through his mind, making his skin crawl. The gypsies were a wild bunch, far more unpredictable than those pesky buggers out in India. At least one knew what one was facing out there.

This lot were damned sinister, with their bewitchery and chanting. God only knew what they did to people who crossed their path on the wrong night. He only knew it was too terrible to contemplate. Give him a damn guerrilla brandishing a spear, and he'd know how to deal with it. Charms and curses were something else altogether. Like trying to run a sword through a ghost.

His uneasiness increased with each second as the thudding hooves drew closer. He could taste the fear in his mouth, and his damn ticker was pounding louder than the horse. He looked around for somewhere to hide until the rider had passed by, but there was nowhere. Just flat ground and a few small bushes that wouldn't hide a rabbit.

It was too late to run for the woods, even if he was certain in which direction they lay. Besides, that would be running toward the gypsies' camp. Out of the fat into the flame, so to speak.

Sweat broke out on his brow as the drumming of the hooves drew closer and closer. He turned to face the oncoming rider, lifting his stick to defend himself.

He could see the horse quite clearly, heading straight at him. Cold, drenching horror froze him to the spot. The animal's dark coat gleamed in the moonlight, and steam billowed from its flaring nostrils. But the sight that held him transfixed was the man seated on its back.

A tall man, taller than most he'd ever seen, sat straight up in the saddle. Dressed all in black, the man wore a flowing cape that streamed out behind him. He appeared to have unusually narrow shoulders. And no head.

The stick fell from the colonel's limp hand, and he began

babbling lines from the Twenty-third Psalm. He'd heard somewhere that it was possible to fight witchcraft with the words of the Lord.

He didn't wait to find out if it worked. Turning tail, he fled across the grass, heading heaven knew where, just as long as it was away from that terrifying apparition.

He didn't get very far before his foot hit an uneven clump and he fell headlong, spread-eagled in the wet grass. Instinctively the colonel folded his arms around his head and braced for the deadly blows from the sharp hooves that would surely stomp him to death.

The grass smelled sweet in his nostrils, and his crazed mind reflected that the fragrance would be the last thing on earth he would know. He squeezed his eyes tight as the vibration of the ground warned him the horse was there. In his mind he could see its powerful shoulders gathering for the leap that would bring those cruel hooves down on his back.

He could hear the thing breathing harshly, then a wild rush of air brushed his hair. Something thudded in the grass beyond his shielded face, and he felt the sting of earth showering over his head. Then, to his utter astonishment, the sound of hooves gradually faded away, until silence settled once more over Putney Downs.

Only then did the colonel move. His heart raced so badly he was quite sure it would explode. His body felt stiff, his legs weak, and he couldn't see his damn walking stick anywhere.

Still fighting the terror that the thing, whatever it was, would return, he stumbled at a half run in what he desperately hoped was the right direction.

Then, right in front of him, he saw the maypole. It had been erected just two days ago at the head of the cliffs, in readiness for the upcoming May Day celebrations.

Blinking at the pole bedecked with ribbons, the colonel staggered forward, his hand outstretched, thankful to find a support to hang on to while he got his bearings.

He had almost reached it when he noticed the odd shape in the middle. Pulling up short, he peered closer at the mass of ribbons. Something appeared to be caught up in them. Something rather large.

He blinked again several times while his recent meal churned in his stomach. The glow from the brandy had long dissipated, leaving only a raw burning in his gut.

Once more the cold tremors of unspeakable horror shook his body. He couldn't seem to tear his eyes away from the body of the woman strapped to the pole, her lifeless form held in a grotesque pose by the silken ribbons.

One pure white band of satin had been wound tightly around her throat. Her head lolled sideways, resting on her shoulder, while her eyes stared back at him, wide and unseeing.

Colonel Fortescue gulped down the bile that rose in his throat. Oh, good God, he recognized her. He had seen the woman only that morning, smiling and laughing as she had walked in the sunlight on the arm of her husband. She was one of the guests at the Pennyfoot Hotel.

Cecily Sinclair hurried down the main hallway of the Pennyfoot, her wide smile attracting an answering grin from a housemaid as she passed by. Cecily felt like smiling at everyone that evening. She hadn't read her post until late in the day, and the letter from Calcutta bearing her son's handwriting had been a pleasant surprise.

But nothing compared to the excitement that filled her when she read the scrawled words, apparently written with great haste. Cecily could hardly wait to share the good news with Baxter.

Ever since she had taken over the reins of the hotel, after her husband, James, had died a year earlier, Baxter had been a constant source of support and sympathy, and at times quite valiant in his friendship.

She thought of him as much more than simply her manager, as indeed he was, having promised James to take care of his wife after he was gone. Even though that promise had sometimes given them cause to disagree, Cecily knew quite well that running the hotel and facing life without

James would have been a good deal more difficult without Baxter's steadfast loyalty.

He would be delighted with her news, she thought, smiling again when she visualized his reaction. Reaching the door of his office, she gave it a light tap and opened it.

Baxter sat at his desk, a startled expression crossing his face when he saw her. The pen in his hand clattered on the polished surface as he shoved his chair back and groped behind him for his morning coat.

"I wasn't expecting you, madam. I do trust nothing is wrong?"

Well used to Baxter's strict adherence to propriety, Cecily ignored his hasty fumbling with the buttons and seated herself on the brocade chair next to his desk. She had deliberately left the door open. Had she not, Baxter would remain standing the entire length of their conversation.

As it was, he sat on the edge of his chair, prepared to leap to his feet at the merest indication that someone might see them alone in a room together and misconstrue the situation.

"I have exciting news," Cecily announced, waving the envelope at him. "Read this."

Baxter leaned over the desk and took it in his fingers. "Is it a personal letter, madam?"

"Only from Michael, Baxter. There's nothing in there you couldn't see."

"Perhaps it would be better if you read it out for me? Your son might not wish his private letters to be read by someone else."

"Oh, piffle." She took the letter back and withdrew the folded sheet. "'Dearest Mother,'" she read, "'I hope you will be pleased to learn that I am resigning my commission in the army. Since the demise of the Russian Navy at Port Arthur, Kitchener's Army has lost its momentum. Life in the military has become a dreadful bore, with little more than the occasional tiger hunt to liven things up a bit.'"

"I would think that would break the monotony," Baxter said dryly.

"Oh, Michael never was happy without a challenge to

keep him busy." Cecily looked back at the letter and continued to read out loud.

"'Anyway, I was interested to hear the news about the George and Dragon being up for sale. I do believe it would be a blast to come back to Jolly Old England and take a look at it. Perhaps I could buy the pub, do it up a bit, and settle down as a publican.'" She glanced at Baxter to see how he had taken the news.

To her surprise he made no comment, so, feeling somewhat deflated, she finished reading. "'I'm getting a bit weary of jumping to attention every time a uniform goes by. It would be smashing to relax in the peace and quiet of the countryside. And to be near you, of course.'"

Baxter's face wore a stoic expression when she looked at him again. "Isn't that marvelous? Just imagine, Michael is coming home."

"That is indeed good news for you." Baxter cleared his throat. "Does he mention the date of his return?"

"Only that it will be somewhere in the middle of May. We have to have a welcome home ball for him, and perhaps invite some eligible ladies down from London to meet him."

"I'm sure he would enjoy that, madam. Though if he intends to live in Badgers End, perhaps London is not the place to search for a suitable companion."

Cecily laughed. "I don't think for one minute that Michael will stay. The George and Dragon is a far cry from the battlefields of Africa and India. As soon as my son discovers how dull and uneventful nights in Badgers End can be, I am quite certain he will change his mind about where he wants to settle down. After all, a man of twenty-five years still has his life ahead of him."

"He does indeed," Baxter said, adding a sigh. "Though he might very well surprise you. He is not used to living in the city, after all. He might prefer the quieter pace of life in Badgers End."

Frowning, Cecily leaned forward. "You don't appear to be too delighted with the news. Somehow I expected a more enthusiastic response from you."

Disconcerted, she watched an odd expression pass over his face, but before she could comment on it, a rustle of skirts announced the presence of someone in the doorway.

Baxter sprang to his feet as the housemaid hovered uncertainly, one hand raised to tap on the door.

"Begging your pardon, madam, Mr. Baxter, but Colonel Fortescue is asking to see you, mum. He's in a terrible state, worse than I've ever seen him."

"Thank you, Ethel. Where is he?" Cecily rose to her feet, wondering what had set the poor man off this time.

"In the lobby, mum. Couldn't get him to budge from there. He's hanging on the banisters, and no one can understand what he's saying. 'Cept he wants to see you."

"I'll come right away," Cecily murmured, sending a glance at Baxter. He nodded at once and followed her closely out the door.

She could hear the colonel long before she reached the lobby, and something about the torrent of words that poured from his mouth chilled her blood.

Fearing the worst, she hurried forward to discover the cause of such agitation. Whatever it was, judging from the hysterical pitch of his voice, it promised to be unpleasant.

CHAPTER

❖ 2 ❖

"Damn gypsies," Colonel Fortescue muttered, looking as if he would fall to the floor at any moment. "They cut off his dashed head, old bean. Riding a blasted horse the size of a mountain, he was, right there in front of me. Though how the devil he could see without his eyes I simply can't fathom."

Cecily's concern grew as she looked at the colonel. He stood at the foot of the stairs, one hand grasping the banister rail. His white hair poked out in little spikes on either side of his head, and one side of his collar had become unbuttoned. It stuck out from his neck, waving like a banner every time he nodded, which was every few seconds.

Sweat trickled down the side of his flushed face and into his mustache. His eyes appeared strangely unfocused, as if he were still on the Downs, staring at whatever it was that had upset him so.

"Colonel," Cecily said, keeping her voice low and soothing, "I'm quite sure it was simply a trick of light. A lost
rider, perhaps——"

"Lost?" The colonel's voice rose to a near shriek. "*Lost!*
Of course the poor bugger was lost, madam. Lost his
topknot, that's what. What!" He blinked his eyes rapidly and
turned his head from side to side, as if attempting to escape
some invisible demon.

Baxter stepped forward and laid a hand on the colonel's
arm. The agitated man shook it off and jumped back a step
or two, banging his head against the banisters behind him.
He seemed not to notice, but shook his fist in the air as he
yelled, "They were dancing around the maypole, madam.
Headless horsemen and dead women. Damn gypsies have
cursed us all. We are doomed!"

In all the years that Colonel Fortescue had been visiting
the Pennyfoot, Cecily had never seen him like this. A victim
of shell shock, there had been times when his behavior had
been a trifle eccentric, even odd, but never this disturbing.
It was obvious the poor man had been severely unsettled by
something.

"He must have overindulged in the gin tonight," Baxter
muttered, as if reading her mind. "He smells as if he's
bathed in the stuff."

Cecily wasn't so sure. True, the colonel's breath could
have ignited a candle, but he had been inebriated on several
other occasions and had never acted like this. Worried that
his mind had finally snapped altogether, she said quietly,
"Perhaps it would be a good idea to get him to bed, Baxter,
before he disturbs the rest of our guests."

"If he hasn't already." Baxter cast a dark glance at the
head of the steps that led belowstairs. "He has apparently
highly entertained the staff tonight."

From the soft scuffling sounds coming from the steps,
Cecily assumed someone had engineered a hasty retreat.
"All the more reason to get him to his room as quickly as
possible," she said, giving the colonel a reassuring smile.

To her relief, he now seemed willing to allow Baxter to

escort him up the stairs. She heard him muttering to her manager as they turned the bend.

"Damn fool nearly knocked me clean off the cliffs. Couldn't help it, poor blighter. Couldn't see a dashed thing without his eyes, now, could he?"

"You should have seen him, Gertie. Went clean off his rocker, he did. You missed a right treat last night, I tell you." Ethel shook her head at the memory. "Poor old colonel, I feel sorry for him. Must be terrible to get old and silly like that."

Gertie, whose breath was restricted by being bent double in front of the cast-iron stove, muttered, "Silly old bugger he is all right. The bloke is proper doolally if you ask me. Belongs in the bleeding asylum." The last word ended on a grunt as she shoved fresh lumps of coal onto the glowing red embers.

"Oh, he's not so bad, Gertie. But he was really upset last night. Wonder what set him off this time?"

"I dunno. Don't take much, does it?" Gertie straightened and sent a baleful look at the glasses stacked by the sink. "Cor blimey, look at that lot. Why the bleeding blazes they have to drink so many different wines, I don't know."

She stomped across the floor, her long dark skirt billowing out behind her. Picking up the glasses one by one, she shook them at Ethel. "What with champagne glasses, port glasses, sherry glasses, Madeira glasses, brandy glasses, water glasses . . . Strewth, I'll be here all bloody day, I will."

"It's that family that got here yesterday," Ethel said, vigorously polishing a silver fish knife. "Seven different wines they had with dinner. And the gentlemen had brandy afterwards. The whole dining room ponged with the smoke from their cigars after they left."

"Oh, you mean the Boscombes. Bloody la-de-da lot they are, too."

Ethel watched Gertie march back to the stove. Grasping the handles of a massive tub full of scalding water, she heaved it off the top and carried it back to the sink.

"Don't that burn your hands?" Ethel asked, flinching at the thought. At nineteen she was a year older than Gertie, and about half the size. Even so, it never failed to amaze her how easily Gertie was able to manage the heavy work without any effort, whereas most housemaids needed help to get the jobs done.

Not that Ethel was complaining, mind you. Having someone like Gertie to work with made her own workload lighter.

"Nah. Used to it, ain't I." Gertie poured the steaming water into the sink, then carried the tub back to the stove. "Not like those bleeding namby-pamby aristocrats, with all their airs and graces. Do some of them bloody good to get their hands into some of the muck we do."

Ethel grinned. "Can't imagine the Boscombes doing nothing like that. You should've seen them last night, all toffed up in their Sunday best. That Lord Sherbourne is a bit of all right, isn't he?"

"He's not bad." Gertie started plunging glasses into the hot soapy water. "It's his wife I like to watch. Real elegant like, Lady Sherbourne is." She uttered a long sigh. "I always wanted to be tall and elegant like that."

"Well, you're tall," Ethel said, feeling sorry for her. "Taller than most women, anyway."

"Yeah, and built like an elephant." She slapped her beefy hip in disgust.

"Well, Ian must like it. He married you, didn't he?" Ethel tried to suppress the twinge of envy. "And why you want to keep on working, I don't know. I wouldn't if I was married."

"It's only part-time." Gertie turned to look at her. "How are you getting on with Joe, anyway?"

Ethel shrugged, hoping her face wasn't turning pink. She always felt warm at the mention of Joe. "All right. So far."

Gertie grinned. "Been behaving himself, has he?"

"Of course he has." Now Ethel knew her face was turning red.

"So that's your bleeding problem. Watcha waiting for?"

"To get married, like you did."

"Has he asked you?"

"Not yet." Ethel struggled to keep her feelings to herself, but she was unsuccessful. "But I think he's going to. I hope he is, anyway."

"Tell him not to wait too long." Gertie turned back to the sink. "You ain't getting any younger, you know."

Ethel hesitated, picking up a fish fork and laying it down again, then blurted out, "Do you like it?"

"Like what?"

"Married life. You know what I mean."

Gertie stood a wineglass upside-down on the draining board. "Yeah, I do. It's better now that Ian's stopped going up to London every weekend. Made me bloody mad, that did. I soon put a stop to that."

"Go on? I didn't know he was going every weekend."

"Well, he ain't no more, is he. About time he settled down and stopped his gadding about, that's what I told him. If he loved me he'd want to stay home, I says."

"I'd want my husband at home with me," Ethel said, nodding her head. "I mean, look at the Boscombes, for instance. I think it's nice that the whole family comes down here every year, never misses. Must be nice to be close like that."

"So Lord Sylvester was there, then?"

"Both brothers were. Both Lord Sylvester and Lord Arthur. And the wives. Wonder what they do with the children when they come down."

"Leave them with the nannies, I s'pose." Gertie twisted the brandy glass in her hand to check for spots. "I think that Lord Sylvester is more handsome than his brothers. He don't look like Lord Sherbourne nor Lord Arthur."

"None of them look alike if you ask me. It's hard to tell they're brothers, really."

Once more Gertie plunged her arms into the foaming sink. "Yeah. Look at Lord Sylvester. Proper lady's man, he is. Always having a peek at a lady's bosom when he thinks his wife ain't looking. Not like Lord Arthur. He's hen-pecked, he is. I can spot one a bleeding mile off."

Ethel got up from the table and began stacking the

polished silverware into the velvet-lined cases. "Well, it's Lord Sherbourne I admire. He looks every inch a gentleman. There aren't that many men what can wear an evening cape and look regal and elegant."

"Not many men wear them at all," Gertie said, pulling the plug with a loud plop. "It looks soppy, if you ask me."

A door banged loudly in the passageway outside, and a deep voice with a strong French accent erupted nearby. "*Sacrebleu,* 'ow can I do my work, if the fools do not deliver what I order? What in the name of 'eaven is this supposed to be?"

"It looks like brandy to me, Michel," Mrs. Chubb's voice said soothingly. The door opened wider to allow the housekeeper's broad frame to pass through and enter the kitchen.

Towering behind her, the chef bristled with anger. His tall white hat wobbled back and forth as he flung his arm dramatically in the air, a bottle clutched in his fingers. "Brandy? I do not order brandy, Mrs. Chubb. I order cognac, no?" He repeated the word, mouthing it slowly. "C-o-g-n-a-c. Not this . . . this . . . pee!"

Ethel giggled, and Mrs. Chubb sent her a scathing glance. "Haven't you girls finished in here yet? Get a move on, right this minute. It'll be time to lay the luncheon tables in a few minutes."

"Strewth," Gertie mumbled. "Bleeding never-ending, ain't it?" She stomped across the floor, carrying a heavy tray of glasses.

"Wait a minute, Gertie." Mrs. Chubb turned to glare at Michel. "I will examine the order that went out, and if there was a discrepancy, I will ask Mr. Baxter to see about it. It might well be that Madam wished you to use the brandy instead of cognac, seeing as how most of it ends up down your throat, anyway."

Michel's face turned scarlet, and his mouth opened and closed again with a snap.

Ethel watched in silent enjoyment as he slammed the bottle down on the scrubbed oak table and turned his back on everyone. She knew what was coming. Michel would take out his anger by slamming pots and pans around, deafening everyone within earshot. This had to be the only hotel in England with lumps and bumps in all the saucepans.

Across the room Mrs. Chubb rolled her eyes to the ceiling as the first saucepan crashed to the tile floor. Raising her voice to be heard above the din, she yelled at Gertie, "Captain Phillips, in room eleven! He didn't come down to dinner last night, and he hasn't been down to breakfast yet. I want you to go up and knock on his door, just to make sure he's all right."

"P'raps he had it sent up to his room!" Gertie yelled back, as two lids clashed together like cymbals.

"No, there was only one dinner went up last night. That was to Lord Sherbourne's suite. So get up there, my girl, and see if he's all right."

Muttering something, Gertie left, and Ethel decided it was time she left, too, before her eardrums exploded from the noise.

Cecily looked out across the gardens, enjoying the quiet peace of the morning. Through the open window she could hear the steady chirping of the sparrows, interrupted now and again by the hollow cry of a seagull.

Her suite on the second floor gave her a view of the Rose Garden and the croquet lawn beyond. She could see John Thimble, the gardener, trudging slowly across the sun-warmed grass, a large sack hanging from his shoulder.

She smiled, thinking how lucky she was to have such a devoted worker. John managed the entire hotel gardens single-handedly and kept everything as neat as a pin. Looking at the pristine lawns, glistening with a heavy dew, and the clean lines of the carved boxwood, Cecily nodded in quiet satisfaction. James would be happy to know that his beloved hotel was being taken care of so well.

She had promised James as he lay dying that she would not allow the hotel to pass out of the family. That hadn't always been easy, and it would be many years before the loans had been repaid and the Pennyfoot secure; but so far things seemed to be running fairly smoothly. Soon the

Season would be upon them, and the hotel would once more be full to capacity.

On her way down the stairs to breakfast, Cecily reflected how fortunate she had been to have at least a few visitors in the hotel during the off-season. With the Boscombes, as well as a dozen other guests, staying for the May Day festivities, her profit would stretch to hire a doorman for the summer.

She had just reached the last step when she saw the tall figure of Lord Sherbourne striding across the lobby toward her. She called out a greeting, her smile fading as he reached her. She could see that he was greatly distressed. His appealing face seemed to have become lined overnight, and his color was ashen.

"Mrs. Sinclair," he said in a rasping voice she hardly recognized, "I must ask you to contact a police constable at once."

Shocked at his pallor and filled with apprehension, she raised a hand to her neck. "Why, of course, Lord Sherbourne. May I ask what is wrong?"

"You may indeed, madam." He cleared his throat and then added harshly, "I have to report a missing person. Lady Sherbourne . . . my dear wife . . . apparently has not been seen by anyone since yesterday afternoon. I am dreadfully afraid that something must have happened to her."

Cecily stared at Lord Sherbourne for several moments in silence, then said quietly, "Perhaps we should retire to the library to discuss this matter."

"Madam, I must insist you call the police on the telephone—"

"I am sorry, Lord Sherbourne. There is no telephone in the hotel. I will have to send a messenger. But first, perhaps you should tell me as much as you can, so that we can be sure the constable has the facts as quickly as possible."

Wiping his brow with his fingertips, the gentleman muttered, "I cannot believe this. I just cannot believe this."

Not quite sure if he meant the lack of a telephone or his

wife's disappearance, Cecily led the way to the library with a great deal of apprehension.

Upon entering the spacious room, she took her seat as usual at the head of the long Jacobean table. From there she could see her late husband's portrait, which hung above the marble fireplace.

Although the intensity of pain had lessened, she still felt her loss keenly enough to need daily contact with James. The portrait afforded that small comfort, and she never missed an opportunity to spend some time with it.

She glanced at the oil painting of the handsome figure in military uniform and sent him a silent hello. Then she shifted her gaze to the man who hovered just inside the door. "Now, Lord Sherbourne, perhaps you would be so good as to tell me everything you know about Lady Sherbourne's whereabouts, starting with the last time you saw her."

She reached for the notebook and pencil that she kept in the drawer at the end of the table. She used this room several times a month to plan the various social activities at the hotel. Two of her close friends served on the committee, and the three of them had organized many a successful spectacular at that table.

She would have smiled at the thought had it not been for the distraught man pacing back and forth across the parquet floor.

"I've told you, madam, the last time my wife was seen was yesterday afternoon."

"That was the last time you saw her?"

"Yes, it was." He stopped pacing and threw his head back to stare at the ceiling. "I kissed her goodbye as she made ready to leave the suite. She had told me she planned to visit the shops with her sister-in-law, Lady Deirdre." He dropped his chin and gave Cecily a haunted look. "That's my brother Sylvester's wife."

"Yes, I am aware of that. So it was Lady Deirdre who was the last person to see your wife alive?"

"No, not at all." His exasperated sigh filled the room. "You see, I had a great deal of work that needed attention, paperwork and correspondence in connection with the estate. If I didn't take on the responsibility of our financial affairs, no one else would dream of doing so."

By "no one" Cecily assumed he meant his two brothers, Sylvester and Arthur. "So you worked on your accounts yesterday afternoon?"

"Yes, all afternoon and evening. When my wife failed to return, I assumed she was spending the evening with the rest of the family, so as to avoid disturbing me. She does that on occasion, when she knows I am particularly busy."

Cecily nodded, busily scribbling down a brief version of what he told her.

"I ordered dinner in my room when I realized she would not be expecting me to dine with her. I was feeling most grateful for her consideration, since I had a great deal on my mind. About ten o'clock last night I finally succumbed to weariness and retired early to bed."

Cecily looked up. "But she didn't return to the room."

He shook his head, swallowed several times, then in an agonized voice said, "No, she didn't return. When I awoke this morning and saw that she hadn't slept in the bed all night, I became alarmed. I immediately went in search of Lady Deirdre."

"And?"

He jiggled loose change in his trouser pocket for several seconds before he answered her. "Apparently my wife had not visited the shops yesterday afternoon with Lady Deirdre. My sister-in-law had not the slightest idea where Lady Sherbourne had gone. Neither did anyone else in the family. I questioned them all. I can not imagine where my wife could have gone, Mrs. Sinclair. Nor can I imagine where she might possibly be at this moment."

The thought had been nudging Cecily for several minutes. Now, reluctantly, she brought it to the forefront of her mind to examine it. Colonel Fortescue's strange ramblings about a headless horseman last night . . . What was it he'd said? *They were dancing around the maypole, madam. Headless horsemen and dead women.*

CHAPTER

❊ 3 ❊

No, Cecily thought, it was too preposterous to consider. And she certainly wasn't going to worry Lord Sherbourne any more at this point by sharing her uneasiness.

"Well, I'm sure there is a perfectly reasonable explanation for her disappearance," she said, praying that her words were true. "But, just in case, I will send this by special messenger to Police Constable Northcott, suggesting that he launch a search. It might be that Lady Sherbourne simply changed her mind about the shopping jaunt and decided to go for a walk or a ride instead. She could have wandered into the woods and become lost, or perhaps been thrown by her horse somewhere—"

She broke off as Lord Sherbourne let out a loud groan. "I'm sorry, madam. While I appreciate your help, and I'm sure the constable will do his best to find her, I cannot stand around here and wait for results. If the police wish to speak to me, please inform them I shall be out on the Downs, looking for my wife."

Cecily stood, feeling desperately sorry for the poor man. It was obvious he was devastated by this. She could only hope and pray that his wife would be found, alive and well.

"Of course, Lord Sherbourne, I understand. I'm sure P.C. Northcott will also be sympathetic. Please try not to worry. It isn't the first time a stranger to these parts has been lost in the woods."

"Maybe so," Lord Sherbourne muttered darkly, "but it is the first time someone has become lost while there are gypsies camped out there, is that not so?"

Again Cecily felt a pang of apprehension. *Damn gypsies. They cut off his head, old bean.* No, she would not let the babbling of a slightly deranged inebriate disturb her. Uneasily she watched Lord Sherbourne give her a stiff bow and then leave the room.

Lifting her gaze to James's portrait, she gave an audible sigh. "I pray that he finds her alive and well, James. The Pennyfoot has seen far too much tragedy in the past months. I am beginning to believe that the Earl of Saltchester left a curse on this building."

James's permanent smile warmed her, as it always did. How he would have laughed at her fancy. He would have been quick to point out that the reason the Earl of Saltchester was forced to sell his country estate was because of his own mishandling of his affairs.

He would also have declared that had the man not been so foolish as to lose his entire fortune, James would not have had the opportunity to buy the mansion, and therefore there would not have been a Pennyfoot Hotel.

Cecily sent her late husband a resigned nod. His logic had always overpowered her misgivings. As always, he had reached out from another world to comfort her. "Thank you, James," she whispered softly.

Then she smiled. "He's coming home, James. Michael is coming home. At least one of our sons is returning to the fold. Perhaps Andrew will follow soon, as well. Wouldn't that be wonderful?"

Feeling a twinge of excitement at the thought, she folded up the page she had torn from the notebook. Then, with a last glance at the portrait, she left the library and went in search of Samuel, the footman.

She found him in the yard behind the kitchen, cleaning the guests' riding boots. Handing him the folded paper, she instructed him to leave at once and take the note to P.C. Northcott.

Make sure you hand it to him and no one else," she told him.

Samuel nodded, tucking the note into his waistcoat pocket for safety. He looked very pleased about the opportunity to leave his tedious chore.

"Tell Ian I'd like him to finish these boots," Cecily said, eyeing the row of muddied black leather waiting to be cleaned.

"He won't take kindly to that, mum," Samuel said with a cocky grin. "Bit beneath a stable manager, that be."

"If he wants his wages at the end of the week, he'll do it," Cecily said firmly. She started to turn away, then looked back at Samuel, who still wore a grin. "You may tell him I said so," she added.

"Yes, mum." Samuel touched his forehead with his fingertips, then strode away, whistling loudly.

Shaking her head, Cecily went back into the hotel through the foyer.

Baxter met her at the foot of the stairs, his square face wearing a frown. "I have just had a word with Lord Sherbourne. He tells me his wife is missing."

"Yes, I know. I have just this minute sent word to P.C. Northcott to launch a search for her." She gave Baxter a wan smile. "I wouldn't be surprised if she's fallen off a horse. If only women were allowed to wear trousers, instead of being forced to ride sidesaddle, the pleasure of horse riding could be enjoyed with a great deal more security."

Baxter coughed. "If you would permit me to say so, madam, I do not consider a horse to be an elegant mode of transportation for a lady. That is why traps were invented. The one good thing about the invention of the motorcar is that it will perhaps reduce the number of women who insist on careening around the countryside on horseback."

Cecily stared at him for a long moment, her anxiety over Lady Sherbourne temporarily forgotten. "Baxter," she said at last. "There are times when you positively surpass yourself. Perhaps I should demonstrate my disgust with your comments by emulating a very famous horsewoman."

Baxter pursed his lips. "And who might that be, madam?"

She leaned forward. "Lady Godiva, of course. Now that would, indeed, be a scandal for you to gloat over."

She had the satisfaction of seeing his neck turn a bright red before she swept past him and mounted the stairs to her suite.

Gertie reached the bend in the stairs and paused. It seemed to take longer than usual to get her breath back, and she leaned for a moment on the banister rail. Only a few more hours and she'd know for sure. Not that she wasn't certain already. She'd lost her breakfast so many times during the last two weeks. If she didn't have a bloody bun in the oven, then she was in dead trouble.

She lifted her head and eyed the next flight of stairs with disgust. Just because some silly old geezer couldn't get himself down to his meals on time, she had to drag herself up two bleeding flights of stairs and down again. In her delicate state, mind you.

A grin replaced the scowl, and she wrapped her arms around her ample waist and hugged herself. Of course, no one knew about it yet. She hadn't told a blinking soul, she hadn't. Not even Ian. Not until she was sure. She could just imagine his face when she told him.

Her grin faded. She hoped she could imagine his face. What if he was unhappy about it? Nah. He'd love it. She was as sure of that as her name was Gertie Brown. Gertie Rossiter. Couldn't get used to that blinking name, she couldn't. She'd been Gertie Brown too bleeding long.

Grasping the handrail for leverage, she hauled herself up the next few stairs. Gawd, she'd have to lose some weight, or she'd never get to the top of the blinking things.

Stupid old twerp, that sea captain was. Probably sleeping off a bottle of rum. All the same, those sailors were. All they ever did was get snoozled on rum and have their way with whatever woman was stupid enough to let 'em have it.

Not like her. She'd done it proper like. Her Ian was the first man who'd touched her, and he was going to be the bloody last. She'd see to that.

Reaching the top stair, she paused until the heaving of her bosom subsided. Second door on the right. She hoped Captain Phillips wouldn't make a grab for her when he opened the door. He'd tried it on Ethel the day before; she'd seen him when she'd gone out the scullery door to empty the slops.

Ethel had been hanging serviettes on the line to dry, and he'd come up behind her, the dirty old bastard, and pinched her bottom. Ethel had let out a shriek that must have had the captain's ears ringing for hours.

That might not have stopped him, either, if it hadn't been for Ethel swinging around with the peg basket in her hand. Caught him a right wallop in the eye, she did. Served him bloody well right.

Gertie smiled in satisfaction as she rapped on the door with her knuckles. That's probably why he hadn't been down to his meals. She just bet he was wearing a dirty great shiner. She was going to enjoy seeing that, she was.

She waited, but no sound came from behind the door. Frowning, she rapped again, and this time was rewarded with the captain's voice. "Whatcha want?"

"Mrs. Chubb sent me up here, Captain Phillips. She's worried 'cos you haven't been down to your meals." She waited through the next long pause, her irritation rising. Drunk, that's what he was. She was sure of it. She lifted her hand and rapped again.

"Watcha want?"

"I just want to know if you are all right, and if you need anything, that's all."

"Drop bleeding dead."

Gertie stared in outrage at the locked door. Bloody cheek.

Came all this way up three flights of stairs, and that's the flipping thanks she got.

Stomping back down the hallway, she muttered fiercely to herself, "Suit your blinking self, you stupid old sod. Hope you bleeding starve to death."

"Where eez Gertie?" Michel demanded, flipping his spatula dramatically in the air. "She is supposed to be beating eggs for me, no? How am I supposed to produce *le grande soufflé* if I have not the eggs ready in the basin?"

Mrs. Chubb winced as a blob of pink blancmange splatted against the kitchen wall and slid slowly down to the floor. "You could always beat them yourself for a change," she said huffily. "I sent Gertie on an errand, and she's not back yet. Mind you, I don't know what's got into that girl lately. Takes her twice as long as it used to for her to do anything. I'll have to have a word with her, that I will."

"Not that it will do the slightest piece of good." Michel touched the pink mound on the end of his spatula with his little finger. "That girl is not in her right mind these days. She is . . . 'ow you say . . ." He circled a forefinger at his temple, and crossed his eyes.

"She's still on her honeymoon," Mrs. Chubb snapped, surging immediately to the defense of her brood. "Too bad you haven't got married, Michel. It might teach you something about human nature."

Michel's mustache bristled. "I can assure you, Mrs. Chubb, I learn far more about ze human nature by enjoying the company of several young ladies than I ever would tied by the apron strings to just one."

"I don't know about human nature. More like the human body, you mean. Here, what happened to that girlfriend of yours you were so daffy about a few weeks ago? I thought you were really in love at last."

"She did not appreciate my sense of humor." The chef held his finger under his nose and gave a disdainful sniff. "She is a prune, that one."

Mrs. Chubb smiled. "I think you mean prude."

"I mean prune. Her skin was all wrinkled." He gave the

housekeeper a baleful look. "That is so like a woman. She put a word in my mouth that does not belong there."

Mrs. Chubb was about to deliver a scathing reply, but at that moment the door flew open, and Ethel rushed in. "There's a lady at the scullery door to see you, Mrs. Chubb."

"Lady? What lady? To see me?" The housekeeper clutched her throat above the lace collar. "Mercy, whoever could it be?"

"She didn't say. She just said she wanted to speak to Mrs. Chubb, the housekeeper."

"Perhaps if you go and speak to her you would find out who she is," Michel said, dropping a saucepan onto the stove with a loud clatter.

Ignoring his sarcasm, Mrs. Chubb hurried through the door to the scullery. The only woman likely to come to the Pennyfoot to see her was her daughter, and she always came through the lobby. The scullery door was used by the tradesmen, and Mrs. Chubb had yet to see a female version of one of them.

Pushing open the door, she stuck her head in the gap to look out. A short, skinny woman stood a few yards away, as if scared to come too close. She clutched a large cloth bag in front of her, and her maroon velvet hat drooped low over her face, almost obscuring her features from view.

Mrs. Chubb lifted her chin. She didn't know this woman from Adam. The poor thing looked as if she didn't have two farthings to make a ha'penny. Probably one of them gypsies trying to sell a dried-up bunch of lavender, supposedly for luck. It was amazing, it was, how many people bought the stuff for fear of crossing a gypsy.

"Yes? Is there something I can do for you?" She'd deliberately made her voice sharp, and the woman jumped a foot in the air.

Mrs. Chubb frowned. If she was a gypsy, she didn't have their usual surly attitude, that was for sure. Most of them would spit on you as soon as look at you. "What do you want?" she asked again, a little louder this time.

The woman moved timidly forward. "You are Mrs. Chubb?"

"I am." The housekeeper folded her arms across her bosom and waited.

"I am so sorry to bother you," the visitor said in a high wispy voice that made her sound as though she was getting over a bad cold. "I am looking for . . . someone. He works at this hotel, I believe."

She lifted up her face, and Mrs. Chubb peered at the pale blob beneath the hat. The woman was younger than she'd first thought, no more than a chit of a girl. Looked ill, too.

Still wary, the housekeeper steeled herself. "So, what's his name, then?"

The girl shifted the bag higher up her body, as if using it for protection. "Robert. His name is Robert Johnson. And he works here at this hotel."

Mrs. Chubb shook her head. "Sorry, never heard of him. He doesn't work here, duckie."

Two large brown eyes regarded her intently. "This is the Pennyfoot Hotel?"

"It was the last time I looked." The housekeeper was beginning to feel sorry for the girl, in spite of herself. If she stood there too much longer, she'd be asking her in for a bowl of soup. Of course, that would never do. Once word got around she'd fed a vagrant, the backyard would be full of gypsies, all clamoring for food.

"I'm sorry, love," she said, gentling her voice, "but there's no one of that name works here. Never has been. I've been here since the hotel opened and I never heard of any Robert Johnson."

The girl started to turn away, then paused, and looked back over one bony shoulder. "He could be working here under another name."

Michel, Mrs. Chubb thought darkly. Trust him to bring his trouble to the doorstep. Poor thing was probably in the family way. "What's he look like?" she said, careful not to sound too accommodating.

"He's twenty-eight years old, not too tall, and he has light brown wavy hair and blue eyes." The girl pinched her cheeks with thumb and forefinger. "He's sort of sunk in here, and he's always laughing and joking." A trace of a smile crossed her frail features. "Always has a smile on his face, no matter what."

Well, Mrs. Chubb thought in relief, that certainly wasn't Michel by any stretch of the imagination. The chef was a tall, dark, and chubby-cheeked man. And he was closer to forty. "Sorry, ducks, you must have the wrong hotel. Try Wellercombe, perhaps the Salisbury, or the Montgomery. They're both big hotels. Your young man might be working there."

The girl nodded slowly, her intense eyes still on Mrs. Chubb's face, as if she didn't believe her. "Thank you, anyway," she said and let go one hand from the bag to drag her shabby coat tighter across her chest.

It was on the tip of Mrs. Chubb's tongue to invite her in anyway. She looked so thin and helpless, poor child. But before she could give in to the impulse, the girl turned away and trudged across the yard to the gate.

Gently Mrs. Chubb closed the door, her brow creasing in thought. It wasn't Michel, that was for sure. But now she came to think about it, the description sounded a lot like Ian.

She gave an impatient shake of her head. Of course it couldn't be Ian. Whatever was she thinking about? Ian was Ian Rossiter, not this Robert Johnson.

A thought struck her, and she dragged the door open again. The girl had passed through the gate and was in the act of closing it.

"Here," Mrs. Chubb called out. "How did you know my name?"

For the first time she saw a real smile on the thin lips. "Robert told me," the strange girl said.

CHAPTER

❊ 4 ❊

That afternoon Cecily climbed the stairs to the roof garden. It had been more than a week since she'd visited the small oasis James had created between the sloping roofs of the hotel.

At one time it had been a retreat for both of them, a brief interlude in James's busy day at the hotel. After James had died, Cecily had opened up the garden to the guests, as a memorial to her dead husband.

At first she had been unable to bear being alone up there, but now she could enjoy it and derive a certain sense of peace from the memories.

Leaning against the wall, she laid her hands on the sun-warmed bricks and looked down upon the harbor, where fishing boats bobbed in the gentle swell. The soft breeze wafted a stray strand of hair across her face, and she stroked it back into place. She breathed deeply, enjoying the

salty fragrance of seaweed, which the tourists insisted on
calling "the ozone."

Looking down, she followed the curve of the beach until
it disappeared around the foot of the cliffs that towered
above the seashore. In another month the golden sands
would be thronged with ladies in light summer dresses and
shady hats. Men in straw boaters would stroll along the
water's edge or sit in uncomfortable chairs to listen to the
orchestra play in the bandstand.

The Esplanade would be crowded with children running
and jumping, mothers scolding, nannies pushing prams, and
the sound of laughter from the Punch-and-Judy show would
waft up as high as the roof gardens to make Cecily smile.

How she loved the busy summer months, when Badgers
End came to life and everyone seemed to be enjoying the
carefree days. Especially the aristocrats who escaped from
the city heat at the slightest opportunity and made for the
Pennyfoot Hotel, safe in the knowledge that no matter how
they chose to enjoy their respite, no word of their sometimes
questionable activities would be leaked to the outside world.

Although the Pennyfoot was the only hotel in Badgers
End, Cecily always found it surprising how many of the
tourists from nearby Wellercombe found their way to the
pleasant Esplanade. One day, she supposed, some enterpris-
ing businessman would build another hotel in this compara-
tively untouched part of the coast.

For the present, however, the Pennyfoot enjoyed a reputation for its seclusion, as well as the excellent food served
in the dining room. Which was precisely why the Boscombe
family chose to spend every May Day in Badgers End.

The three brothers and their wives, weary of the hectic
city Society whirl, took refuge every year at the Pennyfoot,
before the height of the Season.

Cecily sighed, her gaze straying to the top of the cliffs,
over which Putney Downs spread a lush green carpet of
grass. So far no word had been received on the whereabouts
of Lady Sherbourne. Cecily could only hope that the poor
woman wasn't lying somewhere with a broken leg, helpless
until someone found her.

Of course, if she had fallen from a horse, then it would seem likely her mount would have found its way back somewhere. Surely someone would have noticed a riderless horse and raised the alarm? Then again, with the gypsies camped up in the woods, it could well be assumed that it was merely a stolen animal making its way back home. Frowning, she tried to dispel her sudden surge of uneasiness.

She watched a small boy running down the Esplanade, the stick in his hand rattling against the ironwork as he dragged it along the length of the railings that divided the pavement from the sands. A seagull, shrieking in protest, soared from its perch and wheeled angrily above the water.

A flash of color caught her eye, and she leaned over farther for a better look. A woman approached at a fast, mincing trot, the bright pink feathers on her enormous hat bouncing in the breeze.

Cecily smiled. Even without seeing the face, she recognized the trim figure. Phoebe Carter-Holmes was coming to call. And Cecily had better be downstairs to receive her, judging from her speed. Whatever matter Phoebe had on her mind, it appeared to be urgent. With a last look at the view below her, Cecily turned her back on the ocean and headed back inside.

"Where have you been, Gertie Rossiter?" Mrs. Chubb demanded as the housemaid rushed into the kitchen, her dark hair flying from under her cap.

"I had to see the bloody doctor, didn't I?" Gertie leaned one hand on the scrubbed oak table and struggled to get her breath. "Sat for hours in the bleeding waiting room, I did. I swear those old biddies only go there to eye up Dr. Prestwick."

"Gertie—"

"Bit smarmy with the ladies, if you ask me."

"Gertie—" Mrs. Chubb closed her mouth in a thin line as Gertie blithely ignored her and went on chattering.

"Though he is handsome, I s'pose, if you like those kind of pretty-boy looks. Mind you—"

Mrs. Chubb crossed her arms over her bosom. "Gert-ay!" This time her raised voice had the desired effect.

"What!" Gertie clutched her heaving chest. "I was only telling you where I've been. Blimey, you don't have to jump down me throat."

"Why didn't you go to the doctor's on one of your days off?"

"I had to go when he could see me, didn't I? It's not my bleeding fault if his waiting room's always full of boggle-eyed ladies."

"Well, you're late, and the potatoes have to be peeled before Michel gets here, or he'll be chucking those sauce-pans around again. I have a headache now. I don't need to listen to that racket tonight."

"Oh, all right." Gertie pushed herself away from the table and stomped across the kitchen, mumbling to herself.

Feeling a twinge of conscience, Mrs. Chubb softened her tone. "So what did the doctor say, then?"

Gertie sent her a startled look. "Oh, he think it's something I've eaten upsetting me. He took some tests, and I'll know tomorrow or the next day."

Mrs. Chubb narrowed her gaze. It wasn't like Gertie to be so evasive. "Is everything all right, Gertie?"

"Yeah, 'course it is. What could be wrong?"

Mrs. Chubb watched her in silence as she opened the larder door and disappeared inside. Gertie reappeared a moment later, carrying a bulging sack of potatoes. With a grunt she heaved the heavy load up onto the sink and opened the neck of the sack. Potatoes tumbled noisily into the sink, and Mrs. Chubb waited until the clattering had subsided before saying quietly, "Did you knock up Captain Phillips this morning."

"Yes, I did." Gertie rattled around in the cutlery drawer and took out a stubby knife. Grabbing hold of a potato, she rinsed it under the faucet, then attacked it with the knife. "Stupid old git. Told me to drop bleeding dead, he did."

"What!" Mrs. Chubb shook her head. "I'm sure he didn't say that."

"He bloody did. I knocked on his door, and he shouted at

me. I asked him if he was all right, and he told me to drop
bleeding dead." She shot a defiant look over her shoulder at
the housekeeper. "Those were his very words. On me life,
they were."

Mrs. Chubb frowned. "How very odd. He's always such
a pleasant man."

"Yeah, well he ain't blinking pleasant no more. Probably
still sloshed from last night. Ian said he was down the pub
the night before, telling smutty jokes, he was."

"Well, I suppose if he was in the George and Dragon last
night, he could have eaten his dinner down there. But that
doesn't explain why he didn't come down to his breakfast.
He hasn't been down to lunch either."

Mrs. Chubb pulled open a drawer in the table and took
out Michel's steel. The chef didn't like anyone using his
utensils, but by the way Gertie was chopping that potato
about, it looked as if her knife needed sharpening.

"Not like the captain to miss his meals, it isn't. He loves
Michel's cooking. You sure he sounded all right?" She took
the knife out of Gertie's hand and stroked it rapidly up and
down on the steel.

"He sounded bleeding all right to me. I asked him twice.
If he'd been ill he would have said something, wouldn't
he?"

"Yes, I suppose you're right." Mrs. Chubb handed back
the knife, then hurried to put back the steel before Michel
came in and caught her with it. "Still, I feel a bit uneasy
about it. If the captain doesn't come down to dinner tonight,
I'll send Ethel up there in the morning to see if he's all
right."

"Strewth," Gertie muttered and went on slicing at the
potato with vicious strokes.

Mrs. Chubb stared at her thoughtfully. "You would tell
me," she said slowly, "if something was wrong with you, I
hope?"

"'Course I would." Gertie dropped the potato into an
empty saucepan and grabbed hold of another.

Mrs. Chubb had to be satisfied with that.

*   *   *

Cecily arrived in the lobby just in time to see Phoebe barge in through the front door, leaving a wisp of pink feather floating to the floor behind her.

"Oh, thank goodness you are here," Phoebe said with a gasp, upon catching sight of Cecily. "This is all very distressing. I really don't know what I am going to do."

Having become accustomed to her friend's aptitude for bordering on hysterics at the slightest provocation, Cecily smiled and took Phoebe's arm.

"Come, my dear, I'm sure a nice cup of tea will help. Why don't we go up to my suite, and I'll have tea sent up."

To Cecily's surprise, Phoebe seemed only slightly mollified by this much-loved treat. "Well," she murmured, fanning her pink face with a lace-edged handkerchief, "I do adore tea, of course, but I'm afraid it will take a great deal more effort to solve this problem."

Feeling a touch of concern, Cecily ushered Phoebe up the stairs to her suite. After settling her friend into her favorite Queen Anne armchair, she pulled the silk bellpull to signal the kitchen. "Now," she said, seating herself on the ottoman, "while we are waiting, why don't you tell me what has sent you into this state of agitation?"

The feathers on Phoebe's hat trembled. "My dear, I am afraid we have a disaster on our hands. I assembled the maypole dancers this morning for a rehearsal. We are only a few days away from May Day, and those dreadful girls are still bumping into each other and trying to strangle each other with the ribbons. There are times when I would cheerfully strangle them myself. I have never seen such incompetent nincompoops in all my life."

Cecily smiled in relief. "Is that all? You had me quite concerned. Don't worry, Phoebe, I'm sure they will be perfectly fine on the day, and will give their usual delightful performance. Remember how worried you were about the Arabian Nights tableau? Yet it all came together beautifully on the actual night of the ball."

"Until that dreadful python raised its head and caused pandemonium." Phoebe let out a trembling sigh. "My efforts seem doomed for dismal failure lately. If I didn't know better, I would say Madeline had put a curse on me."

"That's nonsense," Cecily said sharply, "and you well know it. Madeline Pengrath might have a reputation for being a witch, but she is a good friend of mine, as you are, and I'll not hear a bad word against her."

"It's no wonder people think she's a witch, what with those homemade potions she insists on dispensing. When someone guarantees to cure everything from a toothache to impotence with boiled flowers and roots, what can you expect? Everyone knows for a fact that Madeline is a gypsy."

"Madeline's background has nothing to do with the person she has become. You certainly cannot equate her with those ruffians camped out in the woods above Putney Downs."

Phoebe sniffed. "Perhaps not, but all I can say is that it is fortunate she is in London at present. Otherwise, no doubt, she would be blamed for this latest catastrophe."

"Madeline?" Cecily shook her head in bewilderment. "What does she have to do with your dancers' lack of coordination?"

A light tap on the door prevented Phoebe from answering. At Cecily's command the door opened, and Ethel bobbed a curtsy in the doorway. "You rang, mum?"

"Yes, Ethel, I'd like tea for Mrs. Carter-Holmes and myself sent up immediately."

"Yes, mum." Ethel bobbed again and quietly closed the door.

"Now," Cecily said, returning her attention to Phoebe. "Perhaps you'd care to explain what you mean by accusing Madeline of disrupting your May dance?"

It was Phoebe's turn to look bewildered. "I think we are at cross purposes here, Cecily. I haven't accused Madeline of anything. It is P.C. Northcott who is to blame."

"Stan Northcott? What has he to do with anything?"

"I've been trying to tell you. I took the girls up to Putney Downs to the maypole for a rehearsal. Before we reached the cliffs, however, the constable met us on his bicycle. He refused to let us go any farther."

Cecily's sense of uneasiness returned in full force. "Did he say why?"

"Only that the area was out-of-bounds. He refused to explain any further than that."

"Did he say how long the Downs would be inaccessible?"

"I asked him that. He said until further notice." Phoebe removed her handkerchief from her sleeve and delicately blew her nose. "I tried to convince him of the urgency of my rehearsal, but he would not listen. The man actually escorted us back to the village. Can you imagine how that appeared? The mother of the vicar, being escorted by a policeman?"

So that was the reason Phoebe was so upset, Cecily thought as she watched her friend tuck the handkerchief back into her voluminous sleeve. To Phoebe, keeping up appearances was a lifelong dedication.

She didn't spend much time worrying about Phoebe's damaged sensibilities. Once more she remembered Colonel Fortescue's garbled account of headless horsemen and dead women dancing around the maypole. And there was the strange disappearance of Lady Sherbourne to consider. And now P.C. Northcott had put the Downs out-of-bounds.

The tap at the door signaled the arrival of tea, and Cecily called for Ethel to enter. She grappled with the problem while the housemaid set the loaded tray on the table in front of her and then left the room. There wasn't much she could do about these unsettling events for the moment. She could only hope and pray that everything wouldn't add up to one more tragedy in Badgers End.

"What am I going to do?" Phoebe complained as she helped herself to a dainty lobster-paste-and-cress sandwich. "If my dancers are not allowed to rehearse, how can I possibly expect them to perform the May dance? They will be the laughingstock of the village."

"You could ask Algie to fashion some kind of replica in the church hall where they could rehearse."

Phoebe laughed without mirth. "My dear, Algie is a vicar,

not a carpenter. He has trouble tying his shoelaces. I don't think he could possibly manage something as complicated as a maypole."

"Well, there must be someone who could manage it." Cecily plopped two lumps of sugar into Phoebe's teacup, then added milk from the delicate bone-china jug. "Perhaps Ian could do something. Let me ask him."

"Oh, would you? That would help, I suppose. Though what good it will do if the area remains out-of-bounds for May Day, I'm sure I don't know."

The same thought had occurred to Cecily. At that point, however, she saw no use in worrying about possibilities that might not happen. Instead she changed the subject. "I had a letter from Michael. He's resigning his commission and coming home."

"To Badgers End?" Phoebe's face registered shock. "Whatever will he do here?"

Cecily lifted her teacup and sipped the hot brew. "He is thinking of buying the George and Dragon and settling down as a publican."

"Oh, my," Phoebe murmured. "That will be a change of pace for him. I hope he's prepared for a rather dull existence after all the excitement of life in the Tropics."

Though she privately agreed, Cecily smiled and said, "I think he's had all the excitement he needs. I'm sure he'll enjoy the peace and quiet of an orderly life for a change."

"Yes, that's all very well, but—" Phoebe broke off as someone tapped on the door.

"Yes? Come in." Cecily watched the door open with a twinge of misgiving. She wasn't normally interrupted while entertaining guests unless it was urgent.

To her surprise and consternation, Baxter appeared in the doorway. "Please forgive the intrusion, madam, but I'm afraid there is a matter of the utmost importance that requires your immediate attention."

His gaze shifted almost imperceptibly to Phoebe, who was in the act of reaching for yet another Swiss tart.

Cecily gave him a nod of understanding. Apparently this was a matter best kept from Phoebe's wagging tongue.

"Thank you, Baxter," she said. "I shall be with you in the library shortly. Mrs. Carter-Holmes will be leaving in a few moments."

Baxter inclined his head and withdrew, closing the door behind him.

Phoebe looked up, the half-eaten tart still in her hand. "I will? Oh, yes, I suppose I should be getting along. You will mention that little matter to Ian for me?"

"I'll do what I can," Cecily promised. She rose, smoothing down her long skirt. "In the meantime, try not to worry. I'm sure everything will work out perfectly well."

To her relief, Phoebe seemed ready to accept the encouraging words. Chattering brightly about the upcoming festivities, she accompanied Cecily down the stairs and actually gave a cheerful wave of her hand as she sailed through the front door.

Wishing she could feel that lighthearted, Cecily headed down the hallway to the library. She had no idea what matter could be so urgent that it needed her presence. But she had a dreadful feeling it had something to do with the disappearance of Lady Sherbourne. The thought filled her with misgivings as she pushed open the door of the library.

CHAPTER

✿ 5 ✿

Two men turned to look at Cecily as she entered the library. The face of the third man was buried in his hands as he sat at the long table.

"Mrs. Sinclair," P.C. Northcott said, standing to attention with his helmet under his arm.

Standing next to him, Baxter looked poker-faced, though a small frown creased his brow.

The third man rose slowly to his feet at the sound of her name. Cecily hardly recognized the man who had cut such a regal figure in his top hat and cape just two nights earlier. Looking at Lord Sherbourne's ravaged features and wild eyes, she knew at once that Lady Sherbourne had met with an accident.

"We thought you should be informed at once, Mrs. Sinclair," Stan Northcott announced in his pompous voice.

His chubby face looked even more ruddy than usual, and his eyes gleamed with suppressed excitement.

Taking her usual seat at the head of the table, Cecily waited until Lord Sherbourne had seated himself again before saying, "I assume this has something to do with Lady Sherbourne's disappearance?"

"It does, indeed, ma'am." The constable cleared his throat, while Baxter's gaze rested on Radley, who had once more buried his face in his hands. "I'm afraid there 'as been an h'unfortunate incident on Putney Downs."

Radley uttered a loud groan. "For God's sake, get on with it, man." He lifted his head, and his dark eyes seemed to burn into Cecily's brain. "My wife is dead, Mrs. Sinclair. Brutally murdered by some madman out there on the cliffs."

The news had been half-expected, but the jolt she felt was nonetheless distressing. "Dear God," she whispered, a hand at her throat. A stark vision of a headless horseman sprang to mind, to be chased away by Radley's hoarse voice.

"What kind of monster would do that to an innocent woman? I ask you, who would want to destroy my beautiful wife? Far sooner I would have it be my body hanging lifeless up there. . . ."

"Hanging?" Cecily looked first at Baxter's inscrutable expression, then at the constable.

"His Lordship found his wife this morning, ma'am," P.C. Northcott said. "She was strapped to the maypole by the ribbons, and one of them was wound tight around her neck. Dr. Prestwick said she was strangled to death."

A tearing sob broke from Radley, and he lifted his face in anguish. "Why?" he whispered. "Why her? She had everything to live for. Now she is gone, and now my life is over."

"Baxter, perhaps you should escort Lord Sherbourne to his suite," Cecily said, unable to bear the sight of the poor man's torture a second longer. "Unless you need his presence here?"

This last was directed at the constable, who shook his head. "No, ma'am. His Lordship is free to go, though I have to ask him and the rest of the family to remain in the hotel until the inspector has been notified of the situation."

"Yes, yes, of course," Radley muttered, rising unsteadily to his feet. "I will be in my suite if anyone needs me."

"I'll have your meals sent up to your suite, Lord Sherbourne, if you prefer?" Cecily said quietly.

"Thank you, Mrs. Sinclair. Though I doubt that I shall be able to eat a morsel of food."

"I'll send them up in any case."

His haunted eyes probed her face for a second, then he nodded. "Thank you. Most kind, I'm sure."

Baxter stepped forward, but Radley stopped him with a flick of his hand. "Thank you, but I can manage to find my way to my suite. I prefer to be alone." Without another glance at anyone, he left the room.

"How awful," Cecily murmured, her heart going out to the distraught man. "Do you have any idea what happened, Constable?"

"Not at the moment, ma'am." Northcott laid his helmet on the table and pulled a notebook from his breast pocket. "Apparently His Lordship took a horse up on the Downs to search for his wife. He was riding along the cliffs when he saw the maypole. Noticing something apparently caught in the ribbons, he went closer to investigate. It was Lady Sherbourne. She'd been dead for some time. Stiff as a board, she were."

"I say," Baster protested with a swift glance at Cecily.

She shook her head at him. "It's all right, Baxter." Turning her gaze back to the constable, she added, "What did he do then?"

"He carried her down to Larch's farmhouse. They sent a message to the police station, and we went and collected the body."

"So Lord Sherbourne removed his wife's body from the maypole?"

"Yes, ma'am. In my opinion it would have been better if he'd left her there, seeing as how she was murdered. I know the inspector will be unhappy about that. But His Lordship weren't thinking straight, and can't say as I blame him."

"So that's why the Downs is out-of-bounds," Cecily said with a sigh.

"Yes, ma'am, until the investigation has been completed. We suspect it were the gypsies what done it. Sort of thing they'd do without a moment's hesitation. 'Ot-blooded lot, they are."

"But why would they want to kill someone like Lady Sherbourne?" Cecily said, avoiding Baxter's gaze, which she knew was boring into her face.

"Well, the way I sees it," Northcott said as he tucked the notebook away again and reached for his helmet, "Her Ladyship was most likely walking in the woods and wandered into the camp, like. Well, we all know the sort of dastardly deeds that go on in a gypsy encampment. She probably saw something she wasn't supposed to see, and they done her in."

Cecily folded her hands in front of her. "And carried her all the way to the maypole to do it?"

"That's why I think it was them gypsies. They'd make it a ceremony, like. Teach everyone a lesson. You can be sure no one will wander in there again after this."

Cecily nodded, still feeling the heat of Baxter's gaze. She knew what that dark look meant. He was afraid she would get involved in the investigation. Considering her past record in that respect, she could hardly blame his apprehension. That didn't mean she would let it prevent her from pursuing whatever course she felt necessary.

"That brings us to one last but important question, Constable."

"H'and what's that, ma'am?"

"I can't help wondering why Lady Sherbourne would be up on Putney Downs, wandering in the woods alone."

For a moment the constable looked nonplussed, then he recovered himself. "I'm quite sure there is a reasonable h'explanation, ma'am. Once we begin the h'investigation, no doubt all that will come out."

"Yes, I'm sure it will. And how long do you think that will take?"

Northcott cleared his throat loudly. "Well, ma'am, at present the inspector is in London, meeting with Scotland Yard. I don't expect him back before the end of the week."

"Then he won't return until after May Day?"

The constable looked uncomfortable. "I'm afraid that is correct, ma'am. Until then I will have to put the h'entire Downs out-of-bounds. It will put the kibosh on the May Day festival, I reckon."

"It certainly will." Cecily unlocked her hands. "There is something I feel I should mention at this point."

"What's that, ma'am?"

"Colonel Fortescue returned to the hotel late last night with a story about being chased by a headless horseman."

Northcott grinned. "Ho, fancy that. Well, everybody knows the colonel is bonkers, don't they?" Chuckling, he winked at Cecily.

Baxter made an odd sound that sounded very much like the warning growl of a guard dog.

Cecily looked at him. "Did you say something, Baxter?"

"No, madam."

She noticed, however, that he directed a lethal glare at the constable. Before the policeman could react, she said quickly, "I have to admit that was our first impression, also. Upon reflection, though, I do remember the colonel mentioning dead bodies around the maypole. You might want to question him. It's quite possible he did see something up there last night."

"I've never made any sense of anything Colonel Fortescue has said." Northcott sniffed and looked down his nose at Baxter. "I think I'll leave the h'interrogation up to the inspector."

Sensing the tension between the two men building like storm clouds, Cecily rose to her feet. "Thank you for the information, constable."

"Yes, ma'am." The constable shuffled his feet for a moment or two, then said awkwardly, "I have to be getting back to the station, ma'am."

"Yes, of course. Do stop by the kitchen for refreshment on the way out."

The constable beamed. "Why, thank you, ma'am. Much obliged, I'm sure." Nodding and smiling, he left the room.

Baxter watched him go through slitted eyelids. "That man needs to learn some manners," he muttered. "He is far too familiar with people above his station."

Ignoring the comment, Cecily sank back onto her chair and looked at him in despair. "Now what are we going to do? The majority of the guests in this hotel are here for the May Day festivities. Once news of this gets out, no one will want to stay in Badgers End for fear of being attacked by gypsies. This could kill the business at the hotel for months. And the Season is only a month away."

"I am sorry, madam, I know how distressing all this must be for you. As indeed it is for everyone. But there doesn't seem much we can do about it at this point."

Hearing the note of caution in his voice, Cecily changed her tactics. "Baxter, do you happen to have any of your wonderful little cigars with you?"

His face stiffened. "You are perfectly aware, madam, that I always carry cigars with me."

"Then would you be so kind as to offer me one? I am in dire need of soothing."

"I would suggest, madam, that a hot cup of tea might be more suitable for the task."

She smiled wickedly at him. "You can suggest all you like, Baxter, but you know how much I enjoy a good cigar. Surely you would not deprive me of comfort at such a time?"

She watched the muscle in his jaw twitch as he fought with his conscience. Then, with an exasperated sigh, he withdrew the slim packet of cigars from his breast pocket and handed it to her.

She took her time selecting one, then waited while he went through the performance of striking a match for her. Ignoring the frozen disapproval on his face, she puffed vigorously to get a smoldering glow on the end of the cigar.

"Thank you, Baxter." She leaned back in her chair to watch the smoke curl up in front of her. "I feel better already."

"Yes, madam."

"Baxter, what is your considered opinion on what might have happened on Putney Downs?"

"I have not formed an opinion as yet, madam. Without knowledge of the information available, I feel it would be pointless to speculate."

"You believe the constable is correct in assuming it is the work of the gypsies?"

"While I have reason to doubt the proficiency of the constable's deductions, in this case I believe it is a fair assumption, given the circumstances."

"What circumstances, Baxter?"

His light gray eyes regarded her with suspicion. "The fact that Lady Sherbourne was alone in the woods, in an area that is well known to be inhabited by ruffians who hold little regard for law and order."

"Law and order, maybe," Cecily murmured, studying the end of her cigar, "but murder is quite another kettle of fish. What would be the motive, I wonder?"

"I believe the constable's opinion is valid in this case. Lady Sherbourne could have stumbled upon some nefarious activity that would prove disastrous for the participants if made known to the police."

This was generous, indeed, coming from Baxter, who had made no secret of the fact that he considered Stan Northcott to be the biggest incompetent ever born—though Cecily had yet to discover the reason for such contempt, which seemed excessive at times. In this case, however, she was compelled to disagree with her manager.

"I find it difficult to believe," she said, "that they would risk a full-scale investigation of their environment if they have so much to hide. Particularly when they apparently drew attention to the deed in such a spectacular manner."

Baxter's frown deepened. "You have another theory?"

Cecily took a long draw on the cigar, letting the smoke drift from her mouth in a satisfying stream. The pungent aroma wafted across the table, and she saw Baxter's nose twitch.

No doubt he longed to indulge in a cigar himself. His

outdated sense of propriety, however, prevented him from
doing so in the presence of a woman, and she had long ago
tired of arguing with him about it.

Baxter's views clashed violently with her own. In keeping with the relaxed principles adopted when Edward VII
succeeded his mother to the throne, Cecily would dearly
have loved to abandon the previously held myths that
women were to be cherished, revered, and intellectually
ignored.

"As I mentioned to Stan Northcott," she said, flicking the
cigar to deposit ash into a silver ashtray, "I would like to
know why it was that Lady Sherbourne was in the woods
alone, after telling her husband she intended to visit the
shops with her sister-in-law."

"That does raise a question, madam."

"It does, indeed, Baxter. It suggests that Lady Sherbourne
had quite a different plan. One that she was reluctant to
share with her husband."

Baxter's eyebrows lifted in unison. "Are you saying she
planned to meet someone in the woods?"

"I think it's a possibility, yes."

"But that makes no sense at all. I have never seen a more
devoted couple than Lord Sherbourne and his wife. It was
obvious to anyone who saw them together that they adored
each other."

Cecily looked at him in wry amusement. "Why, Baxter!
I had no idea you were such a romantic."

She watched him lift his chin and run a finger around the
inside of his stiff white collar. "I was merely making an
observation, madam."

"Yes, I know." Her smile faded. "You are right, of course.
I think everyone secretly envied the rapt attention that they
lavished on each other. I know I did."

"If I may say so, madam, your relationship with James
also generated a certain amount of envy."

For a moment his gaze held her captive. She desperately
wanted to ask him if he was referring to himself personally
or had intended more general terms. She could not embar-

rass him in that way, however, so she merely replied, "Thank you, Baxter. James and I had a very special relationship. It seems so unfair when a strong union is ended prematurely."

"I agree."

Breaking the contact between them, Cecily looked down at her hands. "To get back to the subject. Although I suggested that Lady Sherbourne might have been meeting someone, I did not infer that it was a lover. It could have been anyone."

"True. But then why would she arrange a meeting place in the woods?"

"Most likely because she didn't want her husband to know about it." She spread out her hands and examined her nails. "How do we know that she was in the woods at all?"

After a slight pause Baxter said softly, "We don't know that. It's merely what Northcott surmised."

"Precisely. And until we find out exactly where Lady Sherbourne planned to be yesterday afternoon, we won't know why she was killed or by whom."

There followed an even longer pause.

"I don't know how anyone could know that, except Lady Sherbourne herself," Baxter said in a tone Cecily knew well.

Bracing herself for the argument she knew was bound to follow, she looked up at him. "One other person knows, Baxter."

His expression remained impassive, though the muscle in his cheek twitched in warning. "And who is that, pray, madam?"

She smiled sweetly. "The person who killed her."

"And he or she is unlikely to come forward and announce the fact."

"Exactly. Which is why we shall have to conduct an investigation."

To give him his due, Cecily acknowledged, he held his temper very well. "I would like to remind you, madam, that you have promised me on many an occasion that you would not involve yourself in business that belongs solely to the police force."

"Promise, Bax? No, I might have alleviated your fears once or twice by suggesting I would think twice before embarking on a certain conversation, but I never make a promise unless I am certain I can fulfill it."

His mouth tightened. "I suppose it would do no good to remind you of the possible consequences should you cross swords with Inspector Cranshaw again?"

"None whatsoever," Cecily agreed cheerfully. "So I suggest you save your breath for more constructive comments."

"I am afraid, madam, that any comments I might be prepared to make at present could be construed as insubordination. Therefore I will withdraw, in the hopes you will take the utmost care when conducting your investigation. I trust that you will keep me informed of any developments."

Rising to her feet, Cecily glanced at the clock on the mantelpiece. "It is almost dinnertime. Since Stan didn't feel inclined to question Colonel Fortescue, I think I'll talk to him again, but it will have to wait until after the meal. I do believe, however, that I will dine in the dining room tonight."

"Very well, madam. I will notify Mrs. Chubb." He moved to the door and pulled it open for her, standing to attention with his face a mask of disapproval.

She made to pass him, then paused in the doorway, looking up at him. "Baxter?"

"Yes, madam?"

"I do hope I can rely upon you for your support."

His gaze shifted, resting on her face. "Without question, madam."

She gave him a small smile. "Thank you, Baxter. You do understand I cannot afford to wait for the inspector to arrive in Badgers End? There simply isn't time. The possible loss of business can mean a setback in our attempts to repay the renovation loans to the bank."

"I am fully aware of that, madam."

"Then you will be willing to offer your help should I need it?"

"Of course, madam."

Her smile widened in relief. "Thank you, Baxter."

"Yes, madam."

She passed through the doorway, feeling a great deal more comforted. Just before the door closed behind her, however, she heard her manager mutter, "But that does not mean I have to enjoy the experience."

CHAPTER

6

Cecily cornered Colonel Fortescue in the drawing room after dinner that night. He had just sat down with a glass of brandy and a copy of the London *Times* and looked surprised when Cecily paused in front of him.

"Mrs. Sinclair!" He staggered to his feet, his eyelids flapping up and down at a furious pace. "Jolly good of you to stop by, what, what?"

"I wonder if you might accompany me to the Rose Garden, Colonel?" Cecily said, glancing at a group of guests as they noisily entered the room. "I would enjoy a stroll on this fine evening."

"Oh, I say!" The colonel made a strange grating noise in the back of his throat. "I'd be honored to escort you, madam. Oh, yes, indeed. Spiffing idea, what?"

Cecily smiled, causing the colonel's eyes to blink even faster. "Do finish your brandy before we go, Colonel."

"What? Oh, right. Don't want to waste the blighter, do we? Oh, no, never do. Never do." Shuddering at the thought, he lifted the glass and drained the contents in one gulp.

Wincing, Cecily waited for him to recover his fiery breath. "Are we ready then?" she inquired when it appeared he'd survive.

"Yes, yes," he croaked. "Lead on, good lady, lead on. Storm the battlements, so to speak. Leave no survivors, what?"

Not sure if she was supposed to answer, Cecily gave a faint nod and hurried out of the room before he totally embarrassed her in front of her guests.

She was halfway down the hallway before she realized he wasn't following her. Her long skirt swirled about her ankles as she swung around, then started back to the drawing room.

The colonel stood in the middle of the room, looking around him in a vague fashion as if not certain where he was.

"Colonel?" Cecily said, curbing her impatience.

"What? Oh, yes. Sorry, m'dear. Quite forgot what I was supposed to be doing." Smiling in a befuddled way, he ambled toward her.

This time she allowed him to go first, a privilege of which he seemed unaware as he toddled off down the hallway.

Once outside, the fresh fragrant air of the Rose Garden appeared to revive him. Already the first rosebuds had popped open and were beginning to spread their velvety petals to the warmth of the sun.

Rows of yellow, pink, white, and red rosebushes lined the crazy paving path, leaving a rectangle of grass in the middle with an ornate bench placed on either side to view the blooms.

Colonel Fortescue stood in the quiet arbor, sniffing the air with the appreciation of someone who spends most of his time in smoke-filled rooms.

"Really should get out more," he said, blinking his bloodshot eyes. "One forgets how jolly good it is to breathe fresh air. 'Fraid I don't get enough of it. Beginning to wheeze in the old windbag." He thumped his chest, which produced a bout of coughing that quite alarmed Cecily.

"Perhaps we should sit on the bench," she said as the colonel fought for breath.

Nodding and spluttering, he did as she suggested, landing so heavily on the wooden slats that he rocked the entire seat. After a moment he appeared to realize that Cecily had not sat down, and made a valiant effort to rise to his feet again.

Quickly Cecily sat down next to him, whereupon he subsided with a sigh of thankfulnes.

"I do hope you have recovered from your nasty experience last night?" Cecily said when the colonel's breathing pattern had at last been restored.

He sent her a hunted look. "What? Oh, yes. Was indeed a nasty business, that, yes. Close to coming a cropper that time, I can tell you. Haven't been that blasted close to death since I stared down the throat of a big cat out in India."

"A tiger?" Cecily asked, impressed at the thought.

"What?" For a moment he looked confused, then he shook his head violently. "Oh, no, old bean. Big cat. It was after my kabob. Had claws that long." He stretched his middle finger and thumb wide apart. "Tiger? Oh, no. Had I been that close to a blasted tiger, I would have been his dinner."

Cecily sighed. Attempting any kind of conversation with the colonel was like wandering in a maze. There were so many twists and turns that one became as confused as he was.

"Got close to a wild boar once, though. Dashed painful that was."

Having heard her son's accounts of encounters with the vicious animals, Cecily could well imagine. "They can cause considerable damage when attacking, so I've heard," she said wearily.

"What? Oh, too true, m'dear. Only this one wasn't attacking. Dead as a doornail, as luck would have it."

She needed to get to the point or she'd be there all night, Cecily thought in desperation. "Colonel—"

"Natives had it strung between two poles, carrying it through the jungle. Yours truly was in charge of the expedition, leading the way. Saw a blasted snake on the trail and backed up. Right onto the dashed tusks of the boar. Couldn't sit down on my backside for a—"

He broke off, blinking rapidly. "Sorry, m'dear, you asked me something?"

"Not as yet," Cecily said grimly.

"Yes, well, fire away then, old bean."

She tried again. "I was wondering, Colonel, if you could tell me exactly what you remember about that ordeal you had last night?"

Again his eyelids flapped up and down. "Ordeal?"

"I believe you mentioned something about a headless horseman?"

"Oh, that. Yes." He shuddered visibly. "Dashed extraordinary, that was. Horrible. Enormous black beast, fiery red eyes, breathing smoke. Ridden by this chappie without a head. Can't imagine how he controlled the bastard. Would have been difficult enough if he'd had all his faculties. This poor blighter had nothing above his shoulders. Nothing." Again the colonel shuddered. "Never seen anything like that in all my days in the military. And I have seen more than my share of bizarre sights, 'pon my word, I have. There are stories I could tell you—"

"Colonel," Cecily broke in hurriedly, "I believe you mentioned the maypole, is that right?"

"Yes, yes I did." His eyes seemed to glaze over, and Cecily had the distinct impression that although his gaze was upon her, he saw instead the vision that had greeted him the night before on the lonely, windswept Downs.

"I stumbled upon it, so to speak. And there she was, strapped to the pole. I recognized her at once, of course. It was that Lady Sherbourne. Dead, I'm afraid. Ghastly sight, madam. Absolutely ghastly. Such a pretty woman. What a waste. What a damn waste."

Any loss of life was a waste, as far as Cecily was concerned. As a military wife and mother, she had seen and heard far too much about it. While she understood the necessity of it at times, she would never come to terms with needless slaughter of another human being.

"Can you tell me what you saw?"

The colonel blinked and shook his head. "Just a host of ribbons, all wrapped around the body. Her eyes were open, staring, as if she couldn't believe what was happening to her. . . ." His voice trailed off.

"You say you saw this . . . horse and rider. Was that after you saw the maypole or before?"

"Oh, before, m'dear. Saw him first. I was trying to get away from him when I saw the maypole. Couldn't believe my ruddy eyes. One minute he was behind me, the next he was jumping right over my head. Reminds me of the time—"

"Colonel—" Cecily leaned forward and peered intently into the colonel's flushed face. "I want you to think very carefully. When you saw the horse, in which direction was it going? Toward the maypole or away from it?"

The colonel stared at her for several anxious seconds. "Damned if I remember, old bean. Whole thing happened so fast. Whoosh, over my head he went. Had my nose buried in the grass. All I can remember is those blasted hooves pounding the ground next to my ear. Reminds me—"

"Well, thank you for your time, Colonel." Cecily rose, and the colonel staggered to his feet beside her.

"Think I need another drink," he mumbled.

"That's a good idea. Why don't we walk back together?" The last thing she wanted was to listen to more stories, but she was afraid if she left the old boy out there, he'd wander off and become lost.

"Oh, right ho, old bean. Jolly good idea. Then I can tell you about the time one of my adjutants got his nose caught in a typewriter. Never did trust these newfangled machines. Had a dashed devil of a time getting it off him. . . ."

Sighing, Cecily prepared herself for a long walk back.

The opportunity to talk with Lord Sherbourne came sooner than Cecily had anticipated. She was on her way up the stairs to her suite when she met him on the first landing. At first he seemed disinclined to talk, and she could not blame him for that.

"I was on my way down to the sands for a breath of fresh air," he told her. "I hoped it might help me to sleep. Though I fear nothing will erase from my mind the hideous vision of my wife hanging lifeless on that pole."

In the flickering shadows from the gas lamps, his face looked drawn and white, and his eyes were dark hollows beneath the bushy brows.

Her heart going out to him, Cecily said quietly, "I am so dreadfully sorry, Lord Sherbourne. Having suffered a recent loss myself, I can well understand how you must feel."

His gaze rested briefly on her face. "Can you, Mrs. Sinclair? To be quite honest with you, I am not at all sure I know how I feel myself. Devastated at the death of my wife, to be sure. But there are so many unanswered questions. I can't begin to understand why she was killed."

The sound of the orchestra in the ballroom drifted up to them. Radley's face seemed to crumble. "She loved to dance," he whispered. "We both loved to dance. Now I shall never dance again."

"Lord Sherbourne, do you not have any idea why your wife would be walking alone on the Downs yesterday?"

He seemed to struggle with the words for a moment, then said brokenly, "No idea whatsoever. As far as I knew, she was pleased at the prospect of spending the afternoon at the shops with her sister-in-law. My wife and Lady Deirdre were the best of friends."

"Did they often go shopping together?"

"Not often, but occasionally they would spend a day in the city together."

"There is something that puzzles me," Cecily said, resting a hand on the smooth banister rail.

Lord Sherbourne gave her a sharp look. "About what?"

"About the shopping trip." She heard voices below and looked down. A couple in evening dress were arguing with each other as they crossed the foyer. The light caught the woman's pink ball gown, glittering with sequins and beads as she flounced across the floor with a toss of her head.

Cecily recognized Lady Deirdre, and her husband Sylvester. They appeared to have had a violent difference of opinion.

Aware that Radley had spoken, Cecily lifted her head. "I do beg your pardon. You were saying?"

"I want to know what it is you find so puzzling."

"I was just wondering," Cecily said, drawing an inquisitive finger down the rail to check for dust, "since Lady Sherbourne had planned on spending the afternoon with her sister-in-law, why Lady Deirdre did not raise the alarm when your wife failed to appear."

For a long moment Lord Sherbourne's dark eyes bore into her own. The expression in them made her uncomfortable. "I believe," he said slowly, "you have raised an interesting question. I shall be sure to get an answer to it as soon as possible."

Something in the way he responded made Cecily feel very glad she was not Lady Deirdre.

The next morning Mrs. Chubb was very surprised to see Gertie walk into the kitchen at half past five. "I thought this was your day off," she said as Gertie took off her shawl and dropped it on the back of a chair.

"It was. But Ethel wanted the morning off to go and see her mum, who's sick in bed, so I swapped with her."

"And Ian doesn't mind?"

Gertie jammed a white cap on her head and secured it with a hairpin. "Ian ain't got no bloody say in it, 'as he. I do what I like, and he knows it."

Fighting words, Mrs. Chubb thought as she lined up the silver saltcellars on the table. Ian Rossiter was the boss in his house, and everyone knew it. Everyone except Gertie, by the looks of it.

"I remember, before you got married, your Ian wasn't going to let you work at all," she reminded Gertie.

"Yeah? Well, things change, don't they. Ian loves me, and he knows better than to bloody boss me around. He knows what he'll get if he does." She jerked at the strings of her apron. "Or what he won't get, more like."

Mrs. Chubb peered at Gertie's scowling face. "Everything's all right between you and Ian, isn't it, duck?"

Gertie gave her a weak grin. "'Course it is. Still on our bleeding honeymoon, ain't we?"

Her tone lacked conviction, but Mrs. Chubb knew better than to argue with the housemaid when she was in a mood. "Glad to hear it," she said briskly. "You've only been married a few weeks. It takes a while to get used to one another. You'll settle down before long. Just wait till you've been married twenty years. You'll wonder how you ever got along without him."

Gertie gave a disdainful sniff and disappeared into the larder. She came back with a jug of creamy milk and poured some into a mug. "Was you still in love with Fred after all that time?"

Mrs. Chubb felt the familiar catch in the back of her throat. "Of course I was. Loved him until the day he died."

Gertie lifted the mug to her lips and drank thirstily. "Do you still miss him?"

"You can be sure I do. Not a day goes by I don't wish he were still there at home, sitting by the fireplace in his armchair, feet up and snoring."

"Yeah . . ." Gertie murmured, looking serious. "I know I'd bloody miss Ian if he wasn't here now. Even if he is a dopey bastard at times."

"Gertie!" Mrs. Chubb shook her head. "That's no way to talk about your husband." She bustled over to the sink and turned on the tap to fill the tub with water. "I expect you heard the news about Lady Sherbourne?"

"What about her?"

Mrs. Chubb spun around. "You didn't hear? She's dead. Her husband found her murdered up on Putney Downs. Strapped to the maypole, so I heard."

Gertie's face turned pale. "Go on! Them bleeding gypsies, I bet."

Mrs. Chubb shrugged. "I don't think the constable really knows, but everyone is saying it could be the gypsies. They think she wandered into their camp and saw something she shouldn't have seen."

Turning back to the sink, she shut off the tap. "It pays to

mind one's own business, I'm always saying. I reckon this proves it once and for all."

"Cor blimey, I bet Lord Sherbourne is upset. He was bonkers over her, he was."

"Don't I know it. I feel sorry for the poor man."

Gertie took another noisy gulp of the milk. "Strewth, I'm glad I'm not still courting Ian. We used to go up there on the Downs sometimes at night. 'Course, that was before the gypsies came."

"Well, I doubt very much if anyone will be courting up there again." Having decided that was quite enough conversation for one morning, Mrs. Chubb added sharply, "And you've come here to work, not stand around all morning drinking milk. Wipe that white mustache off your face and get cracking. I need this tub carried to the stove, and those saltcellars have to be filled, the serviettes folded and put out on the tables, eggs to be beaten for Michel . . ."

"Strewth." Gertie banged the mug on the table. "Nag, nag, nag. Get enough of that at home, I do."

Mrs. Chubb decided to ignore that. "Oh, and when you get a chance, pop up and knock for Captain Phillips again. Didn't come down to dinner last night. I'm sure there's something wrong with that man. Never missed a meal before, he hasn't."

"Well, he didn't have it down the George last night," Gertie said, swiping at her mouth with the back of her hand.

Mrs. Chubb paused at the stove and looked back over her shoulder. "How do you know that?"

"'Cos I was down there, wasn't I. Ian had a blinking darts match, and I waited for him in the saloon bar."

Shocked, Mrs. Chubb gasped. "By yourself?"

"No, I was surrounded by bleeding Casanovas with roses in their hands." She laughed as Mrs. Chubb stared at her. "Come off it, Mrs. Chubb. You take me for a slut or something? Watcha think I was doing? Sitting knitting with all the other wives, of course. It was all proper and aboveboard. Ian kept checking on me now and again. Not that I could get into any trouble, mind, even if I'd wanted to.

It was all women in the saloon bar. All the men were in the public bar."

Put out by Gertie's amusement, Mrs. Chubb said huffily, "I wouldn't be caught dead in a public house when I was your age."

"Yeah, well, like I said, things change. Only not fast enough if you ask me. Take last night. Don't make no bleeding sense. My husband can go into the public bar, but I can't go in there with him. He has to be in the saloon if he wants to be with me. But they don't play darts in the saloon, do they? Oh, no. They play darts in the bleeding public bar."

"They used to play darts in the saloon, didn't they?"

"Yeah, they did. But some flipping men complained about women chattering and putting them off, so now they play in the public bar. Where women can't go. What's the bleeding difference, I ask you?"

"It's the way of the world, ducks," Mrs. Chubb said as she counted out the eggs from the basket. "Men rule the world, and women don't. And there is no way any of us is going to change that."

"Well, I know a bunch of women who are trying to do their bleeding best to change it."

"And going the wrong way about it. All that screaming and shouting and chaining themselves to railings. Catch more flies with honey than vinegar, that's what I say."

"Yeah," Gertie said darkly, "but they're making enough bloody noise for people to sit up and take notice. Sometimes that's all it takes."

She stomped off across the kitchen, leaving Mrs. Chubb to deal with the shock of such an intelligent observation from a totally unexpected source.

CHAPTER

✿ 7 ✿

Cecily was pleased to see Lady Deirdre exit from the dining room alone after breakfast that morning, leaving her husband apparently still enjoying a last cup of coffee. Cecily followed the tall, elegant woman at a discreet distance until she had left the foyer, then she hurried to catch up with her.

As Cecily stepped through the front door, Deirdre stood poised at the head of the steps, smoothing on her beige kid gloves. Her beautifully cut gown in lavender chiffon swirled about her feet in the fresh breeze. Framed in a background of the ocean sparkling in the sun beneath a pale blue sky, with the white cliffs rising sharply on her left, she could have been modeling for a Renoir.

Her delicate mauve parasol stood against the railings, and she stooped to retrieve it as Cecily approached.

"Lady Deirdre," Cecily said when the woman straightened, "I do trust I am not intruding. I wish to offer my sincere condolences on the tragic demise of your sister-in-law."

"Thank you, Mrs. Sinclair. I appreciate your sympathy. It was indeed a great shock to us all."

"I can well understand that." Cecily looked in vain for signs of anguish on the beautiful face. "She will be sorely missed by a good many people, no doubt."

"No doubt," Deirdre echoed, a trifle dryly, Cecily thought.

"I trust your shopping trip the other day was successful?" she asked, hoping the aristocrat wouldn't take offense at such a jump in subject. "I'm afraid our local shops cannot possibly offer the sophistication of Regent Street, but I daresay they are unique enough to enjoy a quiet browse. One can usually find some knickknack to take home as a souvenir."

Although milady looked a little surprised, she answered smoothly, "I found them to be quite pleasant, yes."

"You managed to find something you liked, I hope?"

"As a matter of fact, I made no purchases that day." A small frown had appeared between the flawless brows. "It was more a case of window shopping."

Cecily nodded. "Sometimes it is difficult to find just the right thing. I understand Lady Sherbourne intended to go shopping with you that afternoon."

Deirdre's expression cooled visibly. "So I understand. My brother-in-law mentioned that she had planned to accompany me. She had, however, neglected to inform me of that. I had no idea she held any such intentions. Had she done so, she might well have avoided this dreadful tragedy."

"She didn't mention anything to you about shopping?"

"On the contrary. I was under the impression she had been invited to a croquet game on the lawns."

"She informed you of that?"

Cecily wondered if she imagined the narrowing of the light blue eyes that regarded her. "As a matter of fact," Deirdre said in a tone that suggested it was none of Cecily's business, "it was my husband who mentioned it."

Remembering the spat she had witnessed the night before between Deirdre and her husband, the Honorable Sylvester

Boscombe, Cecily wondered if perhaps the handsome, debonair brother of Lord Sherbourne had been a little too interested in his brother's wife.

It was no secret to anyone at the Pennyfoot that Sylvester was a philanderer and sometimes took grave risks for the sake of an hour's carnal pleasure. Could it have been Sylvester who had arranged to meet Lady Sherbourne that fateful afternoon?

Deirdre had already turned to make her way down the steps. On an impulse, Cecily decided to take a chance. "I wonder, Lady Deirdre, if you could tell me the whereabouts of your husband that afternoon?"

She held her breath as the other woman paused, then slowly lifted her head to look at her.

"I have not the faintest idea why it should be any of your business," she said in a voice that reminded Cecily forcefully of the fact she was a subordinate, "but in the interests of clarifying any rumors that might arise, I would like to assure you that my husband was employed all afternoon in the suite of his brother, Lord Sherbourne. I understand they were working on the accounting for the estate. I trust this will put an end to your impertinent questions?"

When Cecily was still forming an apology, the irate woman marched gracefully down the steps and headed at a fast pace along the Esplanade.

Cecily stood staring after her, wondering what the good lady would have to say if she knew that her husband, according to Lord Sherbourne, had not been in the suite at all that afternoon. Which raised yet more questions. Why did Sylvester want his wife to believe he had spent the afternoon with his brother? And if he hadn't assisted Radley in the work on the accounts, where had he spent the time?

Gertie trudged up the stairs, muttering to herself all the way. "Don't know why I have to be the one to knock him up. It's not my bleeding fault if he ain't hungry. Waste of bleeding time if you ask me. Probably got a woman stashed away in his room. That's what his problem is, all right. He's bleeding living on lust."

Hearing footsteps above her, she lifted her head. A portly figure descended the stairs, and she groaned. Bloody Colonel Fortescue. Another stupid old goat. The place was getting to be a blinking loony bin what with all these old codgers wandering around.

"Morning, m'dear," the colonel bellowed as he drew level.

"Morning, sir," Gertie piped back, bobbing a slight curtsy. Stupid old git. Did he think she was bloomin' deaf?

"You are looking particularly ravishing this morning."

She saw his hand move but wasn't fast enough to sidestep the heavy pat on her bottom. How she longed to shove her fist down his ugly throat.

Backing away from him, she bared her teeth in a ghastly grin. "Thank you, sir." She hoped his drawers got twisted in a knot.

The colonel leaned forward, almost knocking her over with his foul breath. "Listen, my dear, if you are ever in need of company, I'll be happy to oblige. Perhaps a stroll on the beach after dark?"

"I don't think my husband would like that, sir," Gertie muttered through her gritted teeth.

The colonel laughed as if she'd said something bloody hilarious. "What the eye doesn't see, m'dear, the heart doesn't grieve over. You are much too pretty to belong to one man, what, what?"

Lecherous old bugger. She'd a good mind to kick him where it would hurt him the most. "Excuse me, sir, I have an important errand to run."

"Yes, yes." His bloodshot eyes rolled over her. "I can think of an errand or two I'd like to run myself. 'Pon my word, I would."

Gertie's stomach heaved, and she turned and scrambled up the last of the stairs, trying to shut out the echo of the colonel's high-pitched cackle.

Near the top she slowed down again, forced by the lack of breath to take it easy. Normally she could have handled the crazy old coot. But after the bleeding row she'd had with

Ian the night before, she felt more like collapsing right there on the stairs and bawling her eyes out.

Her bottom lip jutted out when she remembered how mad Ian had been. She'd have thought he would have been happy to hear he was going to be a father. As far as she knew, at least, he was going to be a father. She'd know for sure by tomorrow.

She thought he wanted a baby. Why would he do it with her if he didn't want a baby? That's what people did it for, wasn't it? Couldn't understand him, she couldn't. Going on about it being too soon, and couldn't she take something to get rid of it.

Strewth, she remembered the last time she had taken something. When she thought she was bloody pregnant. That was before she got married. Sat for bleeding hours in a tub of hot water, drinking gin and ginger. Took days to recover from that one. And she hadn't been pregnant after all.

She was beginning to hope she wasn't pregnant this time, either. Tears pricked her eyes. She'd been so happy about it, and Ian had to bloody go and spoil it all.

She reached the top step at last and paused to get her breath back. She wasn't going to let him get her down. Probably just the shock, that was it. Once he got used to the idea he'd be as happy about it as she was. She bleeding well hoped so, anyway.

She reached the captain's door and rapped on it hard with her knuckles.

"Watcha want?"

"Captain Phillips? It's me, Gertie, the housemaid. I come to see if you want anything to eat."

"Watcha want?"

Gawd, bleeding blimey. Was he deaf? She took a deep breath. Letting it all out at once, she screamed, "I come to see if you want something to bloody eat. Are you ill or something?"

The captain's voice came back loud and clear. "Drop bleeding dead!"

"All right. Suit your blinking self. Don't say I didn't—"

Gertie's mouth snapped shut as a door opened farther down the hallway.

An angry red face peered at her through the crack. "Young lady," the gentleman said in a stern voice, "I must ask you to kindly refrain from standing outside my room screaming at the top of your lungs like a common fishwife. If you must exhibit such vulgar behavior, please be so kind as to find some gutter in which to do so."

From inside the room behind him came a plaintive voice. "Do come back to beddybyes, Poopsie. I'm getting awfully lonely."

The door shut with a snap, mercifully before the occupant of the room saw Gertie's tongue pointed rudely at him.

She went down the stairs a good deal faster than she'd climbed them. She hoped she didn't meet the colonel on the way down—she was likely to murder the ugly old twit. In fact, right then she was in no mood to deal with anybody.

She wasn't too happy, therefore, when she reached the foyer and saw a woman she didn't recognize wandering around, apparently looking for someone.

Since no one else was about at that hour, she could hardly ignore the stranger. "Good morning," she said, sounding a good deal brighter than she felt. "May I be of assistance?"

The woman turned a startled face in her direction. "I'm sorry, I didn't see you there."

Gertie was surprised to discover the woman was much younger than she'd at first supposed. Not much older than herself, in fact. The face under the maroon velvet hat had a pinched look, as though she hadn't eaten properly for a long time.

In the next instant she remembered the gypsies. Surely one of them hadn't had the bloody nerve to come into the hotel looking for free grub?

Sharpening her voice, Gertie demanded, "Were you looking for someone?"

The woman moved toward her, a step at a time, as if she was ready to run at the first sign of trouble. She had big brown eyes and a kind of desperate look in them. Gertie felt her heart warming in sympathy, a feeling she quickly suppressed. No one felt sorry for the bloody gypsies. They were nothing but bleeding scavengers.

"I was looking for . . . a friend. He works here at the hotel."

Gertie frowned. The only man likely to have a flipping woman looking for him was Michel. In fact, she wouldn't be surprised if the entire bloody female population of London was looking for Michel. "What's his name?" she asked, making it sound as though she didn't really care.

Not that she'd admit knowing him, if it was Michel, of course. She wasn't all that fond of the chef, bit of a prig at times, which was a laugh considering he wasn't no better than anyone else. Still, loyalty was loyalty, and no one ratted on anyone else at the Pennyfoot. No matter what they thought about each other. That had been drummed into her often enough over the years.

The woman sighed. She had a soft voice that sounded hard for her to push out. "Robert Johnson," she said, so quietly Gertie had to strain to hear her.

"Johnson?" Gertie shook her head. "Never heard of him. Sorry."

"He could be using another name."

Well, that was possible, Gertie acknowledged. Everyone knew that Michel wasn't really called Michel. He wasn't even bleeding French. Every time he drank too much of the hotel brandy, he'd slip back into a cockney accent. And Gertie knew a flipping East Ender when she heard one.

"What's he look like?" she said, keeping up the game, prepared to lie through her teeth rather than let on she knew him.

The woman raised a hand. "About this tall. Wavy brown hair and blue eyes. He's twenty-eight years old and smiles a lot."

Well, that was a surprise. Wasn't Michel, that was for sure. Nothing bleeding like him. "Sorry, miss. I don't know no one what looks like that."

The woman stared at her as if she didn't believe her, and Gertie began to get worried. She could be a gypsy after all. Could be some kind of trick. She was still jumpy after hearing about the murder up on the Downs. Wouldn't put anything past these creepy bastards. She and the others could all get murdered in their beds, they could.

"You'd best leave, right now," she said, doing her utmost to look fierce. Good thing she was taller than the woman. If it came to a fight, she could knock her block off. Trouble was, gypsies knew how to put curses on people. That made her bloody nervous.

"You'll be in trouble if Mr. Baxter finds you here," she added, beginning to sweat a little. "He'll hand you over to the bobbies, more than likely."

The woman gave her a long, sad look, then, to Gertie's intense relief, turned and hurried across the foyer. As the door closed to behind her, Gertie frowned. Wavy brown hair and blue eyes. About her own height. Twenty-eight years old.

She shook her head in a violent denial. "Nah," she muttered out loud. "Couldn't be. Not my Ian." Even so, she couldn't shake the feeling of uneasiness as she crossed the foyer to the kitchen stairs.

Mrs. Chubb was waiting for her when she reached the kitchen. "Well?" she demanded, crossing her arms over her bosom.

"Well, what?"

Gertie hadn't meant to be rude, but she was still thinking about that strange woman and her description. She jumped a foot in the air when Mrs. Chubb yelled, "Good heavens, child, where is your mind these days? Did you or did you not go and knock Captain Phillips up?"

Gertie gave a guilty start. She'd forgotten all about the silly old git. "Yes, I did," she said, glaring back at the chubby housekeeper, "and he told me the same as what he told me yesterday. Drop bleeding dead, he says. Last bloody time I climb all the way up them stairs to see if he's all right, I can tell you."

"Did you ask him what was wrong?"

"'Course I did. I asked him if he wanted anything to eat. And that was the bleeding thanks I got. He can fade away to nothing for all I care."

"Gertie," Mrs. Chubb warned, rolling her eyes to the ceiling, "that's not the way to talk about the guests. Madam would not like to hear you talk like that, and I don't, either."

"Then you or Madam can go do the knocking up next time. Them stairs bloody near kill me in my state of health."

Gertie could have bitten out her tongue as Mrs. Chubb peered closer at her. "Here, what's the matter with your state of health? I thought you'd been looking a bit peaked lately. What did that doctor tell you was wrong with you, then?"

Gertie turned away and busied herself folding serviettes. That Mrs. Chubb was a little too sharp-eyed for comfort. "Bleeding overwork," she muttered. "That's what he told me was wrong with me."

Mrs. Chubb laughed and patted Gertie on the shoulder. "If that's all it is, my girl, you've got nothing whatsoever to worry about, that is for certain."

Gertie breathed a little easier as the housekeeper began inspecting the wineglasses for streaks. She didn't want to say nothing before she was sure of her condition. She didn't want Mrs. Sinclair looking for her replacement too soon in case she was mistaken about being pregnant. She'd been mistaken before.

She wasn't sure what made her more nervous the rest of that morning, the fact that Mrs. Chubb kept sending funny looks her way, or the memory of a pinched face beneath a maroon velvet hat, describing in a whispery voice a man who sounded very much like her Ian.

CHAPTER

❈ 8 ❈

The crack of a mallet meeting with a croquet ball floated across the immaculate lawn as Cecily paused to watch the game. The sun had long dried the dew. Even so, the refreshing smell of newly cut grass mingled pleasantly with the heady fragrance of the lilac bushes.

It was the kind of day she used to adore as a child, Cecily thought, glancing up at the pale washed sky. Long, warm days with just enough cool sea breeze to keep it comfortable. She could still remember the tingling of sunburn on her forearms, bared for the first time after dreary months of winter.

As the only girl in a family of boys, she had spent hours clambering over rocks and sliding down the slippery grass slopes of the Downs. It had seemed then as if the entire world had belonged to them. Just Cecily and her brothers, and the lazy seagulls that glided so effortlessly from the cliffs and down to the water.

That was before the advent of the motorcar, which could bring people down from London just as easily as a steam-powered train—and opened up a new, sometimes unenviable environment for the villagers of Badgers End.

Cecily watched as a woman in a long graceful gown of white lawn cotton and lace smacked at the ball and sent it rolling through the wicket.

She had hoped to find Sylvester in the group. She was most anxious to find out exactly where he had been on the afternoon of Lady Sherbourne's untimely demise. His blond head, however, was not amongst those milling about the lawn.

Across the dark green grass, Cecily spied John Thimble kneeling by the side of the rock pool. He seemed to be fishing around in the water for something, and, becoming curious, Cecily decided to investigate.

He looked up as she reached him, his weathered face beneath the shock of white hair looking quite distressed. He greeted her with a sorrowful, "Good morning, m'm," and scrambled clumsily to his feet.

"Is something the matter, John?" Cecily asked, concerned.

In answer he held out his soft hat. Inside it, three goldfish lay unmoving, side by side. "Not a mark on 'em, m'm. Reckon they just lived their span, that's all."

Cecily smiled. "It happens to all of us sooner or later, I'm afraid."

"That be very true, m'm. But somehow it seems all the more pitiful, like, when it's a helpless creature."

She looked down at the fish again, but her mind was on Lady Sherbourne. "It does, indeed, John," she murmured. "It does, indeed."

"Yes, m'm. I reckon I'll give them a decent burial."

"I'm sure they'd appreciate it," Cecily pulled her thoughts together. "I don't suppose you've seen Mr. Sylvester Boscombe on the grounds this morning?"

For a moment it seemed as if John hadn't heard her. Then

he lifted his mournful gaze. "No, m'm, I haven't. But I seen his brother, Lord Arthur. He's in the Rose Garden, talking with his wife. Leastways, they was a while ago."

Cecily glanced across the grass to where the tall laurel hedges walled off the Rose Garden. "Thank you, John. I think I'll have a word with them."

"Yes, m'm."

She left him still gazing sorrowfully at the dead creatures in his hand.

Lord Arthur Boscombe rose from the bench as Cecily entered the sweet-smelling garden. "Mrs. Sinclair, a pleasure to see you," he murmured.

Cecily returned the greeting. Looking at his wife, still seated on the bench, she said quietly, "My condolences, milady, on the death of your sister-in-law."

Grace inclined her head in acknowledgment but did not speak.

"Tragic situation, that," Arthur said, shaking his head. "Utterly tragic. Should never have happened."

Odd thing for him to say, Cecily thought. He certainly seemed more affected by the murder than Deirdre had been. His eyes looked even more heavy-lidded than usual and held the kind of lifeless look of someone who had suffered a great loss.

Although Arthur and Sylvester were brothers, one would have had to look very hard to find any similarity. Lord Sherbourne and Sylvester were unalike in that one was dark and the other blond, but they both carried an air of arrogance and supreme self-confidence.

Arthur, on the other hand, was quite different. The middle brother, he was the shortest of the three and stocky. He had not been blessed with the abundance of thick hair enjoyed by his siblings. In fact, he was in immediate danger of losing a good portion of it, judging by the amount of scalp visible beneath the sparse strands.

He had trouble meeting a person's eye and seemed to be always on the alert, as if expecting something or someone to jump out at him from some dark corner.

By the same token, his wife was no great beauty when

compared to Barbara and Deirdre. Her hair was nondescript
brown, and her sallow skin stretched tight across her flat
cheekbones. But she had an air of quiet calm that made her
sisters-in-law's exuberance seem almost tawdry by comparison.

Deciding that Arthur would be more forthcoming than his
quiet wife, Cecily addressed him. "I was wondering if either
of you saw Lady Sherbourne leave the hotel that afternoon.
I believe she intended to go shopping with Lady Deirdre.
But I think something must have happened to change her
plans before she could do so."

Arthur blinked slowly, much as a man just waking up
from a sleep. "I . . . no, I did not see her leave. I had gone
for a walk along the Esplanade and traveled farther than I
had intended. I stopped to take some refreshment at the tea
shop in the High Street before tackling the return journey.
So it was quite late before I arrived back at the hotel."

Cecily glanced down at Grace. "And you, milady? Did
you happen to see Lady Sherbourne?"

Grace's eyes flicked up to her husband and away. She
started to speak, but Arthur forestalled her.

"My wife," he said firmly, "had a terrible headache that
afternoon. She was resting in her boudoir until almost the
dinner hour."

Again Grace's gaze lifted, then fell away. She looked
down at her hands, folded lightly in her lap, and murmured,
"My husband is quite right. I did not see Lady Sherbourne
after breakfast that day."

"I'm sorry," Cecily said sincerely, "this must be a
dreadful strain on you both. I trust you know that the
constable asked that the family stay at the hotel until the
inspector has had a chance to question everyone?"

"Yes," Arthur said heavily. "Luckily we intended to stay
for the May Day festivities, anyway. Otherwise it would
have been most inconvenient. I fail to see what possible help
we can be to the inspector, since not one of us is aware of
what happened. I should think his time would be better
spent questioning those vagabonds skulking around in the
woods up there."

"I am quite sure he will do just that," Cecily said, reaching to pinch off a dead rosebud. "But as I'm sure you know, in a murder investigation everyone remotely connected to the case has to be questioned."

"Well, I certainly hope the inspector makes a quick job of it. It's difficult enough coping with a death in the family . . ." His voice broke, and he had to struggle to finish. ". . . without being treated like possible criminals."

"Now, now, Arthur," Grace murmured.

Cecily thought she detected a note of warning in the woman's soft voice. In any case, Arthur seemed to respond to it, as he lifted his head and managed a fairly passable smile. "Please forgive my brusqueness, Mrs. Sinclair. I'm afraid this whole situation has been a dreadful shock for the entire family."

With one possible exception, Cecily thought, thinking of Deirdre's cool face as she stood on the steps earlier.

"I quite understand," she said warmly. "Don't give it another thought. I don't suppose you can tell me where I might find Lord Sylvester?"

Arthur started to shake his head, but Grace spoke, and he looked down at her. "He mentioned he was going to take a horse out along the beach."

"Thank you," Cecily said. "I'll try to catch him before he leaves. Please let me know if I or any of my staff can be of any assistance to you during this difficult period of time."

Arthur nodded vigorously. "We certainly will. Most kind of you, I'm sure."

"Not at all." With a last smile at Grace, Cecily left them to head back to the hotel. There was one last person in the family she very much wished to speak to. And he was the most elusive. Come to think of it, she hadn't seen him since breakfast.

Instead of entering the foyer, Cecily kept walking around the side of the building and through the big iron gates that led to the stables. The yard was deserted, but the snuffling sounds and pawing of hooves told Cecily that at least one person was in the stables.

She rounded the corner, holding her skirt high to avoid

dragging it along the ground. So intent was she on avoiding the manure that had not as yet been picked up, she didn't see the woman until she had almost reached the stable door.

The sight of her so startled Cecily that her voice came out sharper than she'd intended. "What do you want?"

The woman shrank back as if she'd been beaten, and Cecily felt immediately contrite. She couldn't let the woman see that, of course. Whoever she was, she had no right to be on the property without permission.

Ever since the murder, Cecily had been uneasily aware of the proximity of the gypsies. She had no wish to be overrun by them at the hotel. Keeping her voice curt, she spoke again. "What is your business here?"

The girl, for she was no more than that, swallowed several times in an attempt to get words out. Finally she stammered, "I'm looking for Robert Johnson."

"Well, there is no one of that name here. You are obviously looking in the wrong place."

To Cecily's surprise, the girl gave a violent shake of her head. "No, I am not. He works here at the Pennyfoot Hotel." She looked around in a rather a vague way. "This yard does belong to the Pennyfoot Hotel, doesn't it?"

"Yes, it does, but—"

"Then he works here."

Cecily drew herself up to her full height. "Young lady, I happen to own this hotel, and I can assure you no one of that name—"

"You are Mrs. Cecily Sinclair."

Cecily closed her mouth with care. After studying the young woman's frail features for a moment, she said quietly, "And who are you?"

"Don't matter."

"It does to me. How do you know my name?"

One shoulder lifted in the ragged dress. "I know all the names at the Pennyfoot."

"And who gave you this information?"

"Robert Johnson."

Cecily's thought strayed to Michel. "Perhaps you'd better describe him to me."

At first she felt relief as she listened to the halting description. It certainly wasn't Michel. But then as she listened, she felt a gnawing uneasiness. It did sound very much like Ian Rossiter.

"I think perhaps you should look for your Robert Johnson in the town," Cecily said firmly as she took the girl's arm and began to lead her toward the gate.

She felt quite perturbed when the young woman yanked her arm from her grip. Independence was all very well when one had the means to support it. This poor soul looked as if she hadn't eaten in weeks.

She was tempted to ask her in, but if this fragile-looking waif was a gypsy, Cecily knew she would be inviting a lot of trouble onto her doorstep. How she wished Madeline were here. She'd know how to handle this situation better than anyone.

"I'll be happy to make some inquiries for you," she said as she walked purposefully over to the gate and held it open. "Where can I get in touch with you, in the event I discover this man for whom you are looking?"

"You can't, I live in London," the woman said, looking defiant. "But I'll be back. 'Cos I know he's here, and no one ain't going to stop me finding him."

"My dear," Cecily said gently, "if I have someone working in this establishment by the name of Robert Johnson, rest assured I shall ferret him out. And you shall be the first to know of it. But it would help if you gave me your name."

For a long moment the girl looked at her with dark soulful eyes. Then without a word she turned and walked through the gate.

Frowning, Cecily watched her disappear around the corner of the building. How very strange, she thought. Then, with a shake of her head, she dismissed the puzzle. Right then she had more pressing worries on her mind.

Hurrying back across the yard, she reached the stable doors and pulled them open. It was quite dark inside, and it took her a moment or two to locate a figure at the far end of the stables. His back curved in an arch as he bent low over a horse's hoof resting on his knees.

Hitching up her skirt, Cecily stepped over the pile of horse dung inside the door and hurried down toward the stable hand. To her surprise she saw it was Ian. He held a thin knife in his hand and was digging stones out of the hoof while its owner stood patiently waiting.

"Isn't Samuel supposed to be doing that?" she asked as Ian dropped the hoof and touched his forehead with his fingers in greeting.

"Yes, mum, but one of the guests wanted a ride into the High Street, so Samuel took one of the traps."

Cecily frowned. "He could have taken on that task when he returned. A stable manager surely has more important things to take care of, like supervising a cleanup of the yard to begin with."

"Sorry, m'm. I haven't had the chance to get out there yet."

Ian seemed ill at ease, and again Cecily thought about the young woman asking questions. "Well, do take care of it as soon as possible. Now that the weather is warming up, it is most important to keep the yard and stables clean at all times."

"Yes, mum. I'll see that one of the hands gets on it straight away." Ian shifted on his feet, his gaze straying to the door behind her.

"Now, perhaps you can tell me if Lord Sylvester Boscombe has taken a ride yet this morning?"

"Yes, mum. He left about half an hour ago. Said he was going along the beach and would be back for lunch."

"Yes, well, it must be getting close to that time now. I had better get back to the dining room and make sure everything is ready." She gave Ian a stern look. "You will take care of the yard as soon as possible, won't you, Ian? I would hate for Mr. Baxter to see it looking like that. And if you don't clean it up very soon, he is going to be able to smell it from his office. As, no doubt, will a great number of our guests."

"Yes, mum, I'll do it right away."

"Good. Ask John Thimble if he needs any fertilizer. The

rosebushes are beginning to sprout." She started to turn away, then as an afterthought turned back to find Ian's anxious gaze still on her. "Ian," she said carefully, "have you by any chance heard of a man by the name of Robert Johnson?"

She watched the stable manager's prominent Adam's apple slide up and down as he swallowed. "No, mum," he said, vigorously shaking his head. "I ain't never heard of no one with that name. On me life, I haven't."

"Well, there was a young lady looking for someone of that name. You will let me know if you should hear of him? Perhaps when you're down at the George and Dragon, you could ask about him?"

"Yes, mum, I'll certainly do that, mum."

"Thank you." Cecily turned again to leave, certain now that Ian knew more than he was telling. She just hoped it didn't mean more trouble. She had quite enough to handle as it was.

CHAPTER

❖ 9 ❖

Baxter was in the foyer when Cecily entered the hotel again. He and Mrs. Chubb were discussing the shortfall of the last order of bedsheets from the drapers.

"I can assure you, Mrs. Chubb," Baxter said as Cecily approached the two of them, "I most certainly did write down ten pairs of sheets and ten of pillowcases. I can't imagine why they would not match the numbers. After all, if one has a pair of double sheets, it would seem to be obvious one would also need a pair of pillowcases."

The housekeeper nodded in agreement. "Yes, well, apparently not everyone is as astute as you are, Mr. Baxter. As it is, we received only five pairs of pillowcases."

Baxter caught sight of Cecily and rolled his eyes to the ceiling. "Very well. I will see that the mistake is rectified. I will also peruse the invoice and make sure we have not been charged for the missing pillowcases."

"Thank you, Mr. Baxter. Much obliged." Mrs. Chubb smiled at Cecily. "Mum," she murmured. Without waiting for a reply, she marched across the foyer to the kitchen stairs, the black ribbons of her cap bouncing on her plump shoulders.

"I shall have to send Samuel with a message," Baxter said as Cecily accompanied him along the hallway.

"It's a shame you didn't know about the discrepancy earlier. I do believe Samuel took someone into the High Street just a little while ago. It would have saved him a trip."

Baxter groaned. "We seem to spend more time getting from one place to another than we do achieving the desired result when we get there." He paused at the door to his office. "Maybe we should consider purchasing a motorcar. It would save considerable time over harnessing a horse and trap each time we need an errand run."

"And who would drive it?" Cecily asked innocently, knowing full well the reasoning that lay behind Baxter's supposedly irrelevant suggestion.

He cleared his throat and stretched his neck above his white collar. "I would be happy to take instruction, madam, in the event a driver is needed."

Cecily pretended to look shocked. "Why, Baxter, I wouldn't dream of subjecting you to such lowly employment. The very idea of my hotel manager resorting to running common errands is unthinkable."

His gray eyes glinted at her. "I run errands now, madam, on foot."

"Ah, yes, those befitting a man of your station. I do believe that with the use of a motorcar, however, the errands would also include transporting guests to and from the hotel. That is more the work of a footman, Baxter. Certainly not that of a hotel manager."

His disappointment could be clearly detected on his face. "Yes, madam. As you say."

Cecily laughed and patted his arm. "Take that stuffy look off your face, Bax. I am quite sure that we are not in a position to afford a motorcar."

"I am afraid you are right. Let us just say I was indulging in a little daydreaming."

"In any case, perhaps it would be less expensive over time if we had a telephone service put into the hotel. That way we could simply put a call through instead of having to go in person."

"Always supposing the person you wish to contact also has a telephone."

Cecily sighed. "True. These things do tend to get complicated, don't they?"

"Yes, madam. And speaking of finances, I had better locate the whereabouts of that invoice, before the thought of it goes out of my mind."

He pushed the door open and would have passed through, but he paused as Cecily said quickly, "Can you spare me a moment, Baxter? I'd like to have a word with you."

His right eyebrow twitched as he looked down at her. Baxter had never felt comfortable about her being in his office alone with him. The library was a little better, since it was larger, and available to the guests. Even then, he fidgeted most of the time they were alone together.

Cecily often wondered how Baxter would go about courting a woman, since he was so concerned about the proper etiquette. In fact, she often wondered if he ever had courted a woman. She tried not to entertain too many thoughts on that particular subject.

Now that James had been dead for more than a year, she was beginning to miss the close male companionship that marriage provided, both physical and emotional. The merest idea of Baxter being in that role, particularly with herself in mind, was both disturbing and titillating.

She jumped when Baxter said, "May I ask what you have in mind, madam?"

Confused, she was aghast to think he might have read her thoughts. "I beg your pardon?"

"I was merely wondering if the purpose of your visit to my office was to purloin one of my cigars. If so, I should remind you that it is close to the lunch hour. It is not healthy to smoke a cigar shortly before eating."

Relieved, Cecily uttered a short laugh. "Oh, piffle, Baxter. I don't want one of your cigars. Not at this moment, in any case. Perhaps later?"

Disapproval flicked across his face. "Then might I ask why you wish to speak with me?"

"If you allow me into the office, I will be happy to tell you."

After a second's hesitation, he stood back and held out his hand in invitation. "After you, madam."

"Thank you." She swept into the office and sat down on a chair.

Leaving the door ajar, Baxter crossed to his desk and stood there, fidgeting with some of the papers lying in the wooden tray.

Cecily watched him for a moment, until he looked up, his face turning pink to find her gaze on him.

"How can I be of assistance, madam?"

"You can tell me if you have ever heard of a man by the name of Robert Johnson."

He looked surprised, then gave it some thought, finally shaking his head. "No, I can't say that I have ever heard of him. Is he a resident of Badgers End?"

"According to a young lady I found loitering near the stables, he works here at this hotel."

"We have no one of that name working here." Baxter started to sit down, remembered his manners, and remained standing. "How very extraordinary. Did she say in what position he is employed?"

"You know," Cecily said thoughtfully, "now that you mention it, that was something I should have asked the young lady. Possibly she would have refused to answer anyway. She seemed very reluctant to give away too much information. She wouldn't tell me her name, for instance."

Baxter frowned. "It sounds as if she is up to no good, in my opinion."

"Well, I must admit I was of the same opinion at first." Cecily leaned back in her chair, remembering the anxious expression on the stranger's thin face. "But after speaking with her, I felt a certain sympathy toward her. She appeared to be very undernourished and not in the best of health."

"Most likely a gypsy," Baxter said sharply. "I really must warn you to be extremely careful. I am sure I do not have to remind you of the dreadful plight of Lady Sherbourne."

"No, you do not have to remind me. As you well know, I have thought of little else these past two days. Not only am I anxious to have the investigation over before the May Day festivities, there is also the fact that my son is due to arrive any day now. I wouldn't wish this kind of welcome to his new home."

Again she noticed the rather odd expression cross his face when she mentioned Michael's homecoming. She was about to question him on it when he spoke.

"Or perhaps you are worried he might forbid you to continue with this unfortunate insistence of yours on taking matters into your own hands?"

"Piffle." Cecily lifted her chin. "My son has no authority to tell me what to do or what not to do." Though that probably wouldn't stop him from attempting to do just that, she acknowledged inwardly.

"In any case," she added, "I fail to see how this young lady can have any connection to the murder. In fact, I am quite sure the woman did not come from the gypsy encampment. She told me herself she lived in London."

"If you'll permit me to say so, madam, a gypsy's word is suspect at best."

Cecily met his gaze with a frown. "I do detest the way we tend to tar a certain group of people with the same brush. While I'm sure that there's a certain element of miscreants in the gypsy community, as there is in any society, I don't believe that each and every one of them is the criminal most people believe them to be."

"I fear you are prejudiced in their favor, taking into account your friendship with Miss Pengrath. It is well known that the element of miscreants to which you refer is far greater in the gypsy community than in a village the size of Badgers End. Or, I might add, a town the size of Wellercombe, no doubt."

Cecily looked at him in surprise. "My, my, you are a little vindictive today, are you not?"

A patch of red quickly spread over his neck. "My apologies, madam," he said stiffly. "I do feel compelled, however, to point out the dangers of venturing into such an iniquitous establishment. I am fully aware of your tendency to take matters into your own hands when swept away by the excitement of an investigation into business that does not concern you."

Understanding the anxiety behind his rather pompous attitude, Cecily smiled. "Now, you know very well, Baxter, I would not venture into any questionable territory without at the very least confiding in you, and even less likely to do so without the benefit of your company."

Looking vastly unhappy, he muttered, "I sincerely trust, madam, that you will have no need to venture into any place of that nature."

Cecily rose and headed for the door. Reaching it, she turned back to look at him. "I echo those sentiments, Baxter. You may be assured of that."

She left him standing there looking after her, her heart warmed by his concern. There were times when she believed that he really cared about her, and that his promise to James was not necessarily the reason for his protectiveness. The thought kept a smile on her lips for quite a while.

As Cecily left the dining room, after enjoying a fresh lobster salad for lunch, she saw Colonel Fortescue waiting for her in the hallway, his blotchy face creased in anxiety.

"I say, old bean," he muttered behind his hand, "you don't suppose that poor blighter lost his head somewhere in the village, do you?"

It took her a moment to realize he was talking about the horseman he saw the night before the murder was discovered. "I doubt he lost his head at all, Colonel," she assured him. "I do believe it could have been a trick of the light that caused you to think he was headless."

"Oh, no, madam, no, indeed. I am positive of what I saw. I see the ghastly sight over and over again in my nightmares.

Cape flowing behind him, those skinny shoulders, and absolutely no head. None at all."

He hiccupped loudly and covered his mouth with the back of his hand. "'Scuse me, m'dear. Must have been the head cheese I had for lunch."

It was more likely the gin with which he'd washed it down, Cecily thought. "Did you notice the rider's hands?" she asked as he sent a furtive glance up the hallway.

"Hands?" He looked confused. "Oh, he had hands, old bean. Couldn't have guided the horse, could he, without hands? Dashed impossible, I should say. Unless he used his knees. I remember once—"

"Can you remember," Cecily said patiently, "if they were large hands like a man's, or small like a woman's?"

The colonel took a step backward and collided with the wall. "Great Scott, madam. You are surely not suggesting the rider could have been a woman?" His eyelids flapped up and down at an alarming rate. "Perish the thought."

"I was just wondering," Cecily said, "if the rider had no head, how you could be so certain it was a man?"

The colonel cleared his throat several times and ended on another hiccup. "He wore trousers," he said at last.

"A woman could have worn trousers."

The colonel stared at her, his bloodshot eyes growing wide. "By Jove, madam," he said in a hoarse whisper, "I never thought of that."

"So what about the hands?" Cecily asked, not really expecting too much from his answer.

"Dashed if I know, old bean. I wasn't looking at his hands. I was looking where his head should have been. Or hers." He sent her a startled look. "Good lord. There could be a woman's head rolling around somewhere. That would be even more ghastly. Unless it fell in the sea and floated away. I can just see it now, long hair floating on the waves . . ."

Cecily smiled. "I wouldn't worry about it, Colonel. I'm sure it will surface somewhere."

"That's what I'm afraid of." He peered down the hallway

again in that furtive manner, as if assuring himself no one was within earshot. "They shrink them, you know."

It was Cecily's turn to be confused. "Who shrinks what, Colonel?"

"Heads. Those little buggers out in the Tropics. Shrink heads. You don't think they are coming over here looking for new supplies, do you?"

"No," Cecily said kindly. "I'm quite sure that isn't the case, Colonel."

"No, you are right, of course. Damn gypsies, that's what it is. Put a curse on the poor blighter. Dashed bad luck, I call it. From now on I suggest you stay clear of the Downs. Hate to see you coming home with your noggin missing. Make it blasted awkward to drink, what?"

"It would indeed, Colonel," Cecily assured him. "Now, if you will excuse me, I have an errand to run."

He nodded in an absentminded way and toddled off, still muttering to himself about shrunken heads.

Cecily waited until he was clear of the lobby before crossing it herself. She needed to talk to John Thimble about the rosebushes. And she desperately needed some fresh air after all that talk of headless horsemen, or women, and shrunken heads.

She found John in the Rose Garden, pruning her precious rosebushes. "Did Ian ask you about the fertilizer?" she asked him as he straightened his permanent stoop as best he could.

"Yes, m'm. I told him I'd dig a pit for it this evening, and he could fill it then. Less chance of the smell carrying to the courtyard that way."

"Very good, John. I would hate to offend any of our guests."

"Oh, I'll take good care of that, m'm, be you sure of that."

"Thank you, John." She hesitated, then decided to ask him anyway. "John, have you ever heard of a man by the name of Robert Johnson?"

The gardener scratched his forehead beneath the floppy

brim of his hat. "Can't say as how I have, m'm. Not from
around these parts, anyhow."

"Well, that's all right. It isn't important." Cecily cast an
appraising eye along the neat rows of bushes. "I think the
roses are going to be quite colorful this year, now that we've
added the crimsons."

"Yes, m'm. Indeed they will. Plenty to look at for those
who like to sit a while."

Cecily bent over a yellow bush and sniffed. "This was
one of James's favorites. I always think of him when I see
a yellow rose."

"Yes, m'm." His eyes filled with sympathy when he
looked at her, but he said nothing.

"It's nice that the guests can enjoy the roses, too," Cecily
said, giving him a smile. "James would be most gratified to
know that."

"Yes, m'm. I'm sure he would. Lots of people sit in this
here garden. Like the Lady Grace. Two days ago, it were.
Sat here nigh on all afternoon, she did."

"Two days ago?" Cecily frowned. "Are you sure?"

"Yes, m'm. Sure as I'll ever be. It was the day I cut the
grass on the croquet lawn. Took me all afternoon. Every
time I passed by the garden I looked in, and there she was,
just sitting staring at the rosebuds. Too bad it weren't next
month. They'll be a right picture then, all out in blossom."

"Well, I'm sure there will be other guests here by then
who will enjoy them just as much."

John gave her one of his rare smiles. "Reckon you be
right, m'm."

"Thank you, John," Cecily said with a last wistful look at
the bushes. "I am happy to see you taking such good care of
the grounds. I don't know what we'd do without you. I'm
sure I don't."

He dropped his face and touched the brim of his hat.
"Thank you, m'm. I enjoy my work. Plants and such, they
are my friends. Don't have much time for people."

"I know," Cecily said softly. "Sometimes I wonder if you
don't have the best of way of looking at things. But then I
think that without pain we can't have the joy, either."

Leaving him to his beloved garden, she headed once more back to the hotel. She needed to talk to Lady Grace again. She very much wanted to know why the quiet woman had told her husband she was lying down that afternoon with a bad headache, when in fact she had been sitting in the Rose Garden.

It would seem that there were many ripples beneath the surface of the Boscombe family. It would be most interesting, Cecily told herself, to discover from where they stemmed.

Baxter's warning seemed to echo in her mind as she reached the steps of the hotel. He needn't worry. She had no intention of wandering up onto the Downs alone. Indeed, she would give a very great deal to know why Lady Sherbourne had done so.

As if in answer to her thoughts, she saw the figure of a tall, blond man leaning against the railings at the edge of the sands. Finally she'd have a chance to talk to Sylvester Boscombe. And she couldn't wait to do exactly that.

CHAPTER

❈10❈

Cecily waited for a horse and trap to pass before crossing the road to the railings. Sylvester stood a few yards away, his elbows leaning on the railing. As she walked toward him she could tell from the way he gazed at his clasped hands that he had a great deal on his mind.

She was about to call out to him when a commotion in the street behind her attracted her attention. Spinning around, she watched in dismay as a young lad, legs tangled in the bicycle on the ground beneath him, struggled to avoid the prancing hooves of the horse with which he had apparently collided.

Cecily was even more distressed to see it was her own trap, with Samuel hauling on the reins in a desperate attempt to control the rearing animal.

She started forward just as Baxter charged through the door of the hotel and down the steps. With admirable disregard for his own safety, he leaped for the chestnut's bridle and fought the frightened horse for a moment before dragging the entire contraption away from the terrified boy.

Cecily stooped to help the child, who was more frightened than hurt. Righting the bicycle, she scolded him gently for not paying attention.

"One day," she told him, "there will be many, many motor cars driving down this road. Should you not pay attention and tangle with one of those, you would suffer a far worse injury than a bruised knee."

The child answered with a scared nod, then sped away without looking back.

A small group of people stood on the pavement watching Baxter as he quieted the horse. After a word or two with Samuel, he started back toward her.

"I do hope the boy wasn't hurt?" he asked, his face a mask of anxiety.

She smiled up at him, a faint stirring of pride warming her. "The child has nothing worse than a bruise or two. He has you to thank for that. You were quite magnificent, Baxter. I am most impressed by your quick thinking."

He looked down at her, his face impassive, though his eyes told her he was touched by her praise. "Thank you, madam. One does what one has to do."

"That is what I admire most about you, Baxter. You are always there when needed."

"I try to be, madam."

"Yes," she said softly. "I know."

For a moment something else gleamed in his eyes; then with a slight nod he spun around and headed briskly for the steps of the hotel.

With a sigh Cecily glanced over at the railings.

Sylvester had disappeared.

He hadn't returned to the hotel, for she would have seen him pass her. Neither was he on the Esplanade. She could see the full length of it, and he could hardly have walked out of sight in that short time. He had to be farther down the beach, below the Esplanade.

Crossing the road again, Cecily peered over the railings.

A group of children played on the sand, watched over by a nanny, while an elderly couple strolled along the water's edge. A man and a woman walked a dog at the foot of the cliffs. Of Sylvester there was no sign. Once more he had eluded her.

Phoebe stood and surveyed the makeshift maypole that had been erected, over Algie's objections, behind the church. The pole had been donated by one of the choirboys' fathers. He used it to chase the starlings out of his thatched roof.

His wife had donated strips of fabric, torn from an old sheet, to serve as ribbons. They were tied to a bicycle wheel, which was then lashed to the pole.

The whole thing looked cumbersome and top-heavy, but in a pinch it would serve the purpose, Phoebe decided. Of course, if this dreadful business of the murder wasn't over by Friday, then there would be no May dance.

But Phoebe was nothing if not optimistic, particularly where her organized events were concerned. It seemed that each time she had a crisis and worried herself silly over it, no matter how disastrous things appeared, something always happened to pull it all together at the last minute.

With the exception of that dreadful business with the snake, of course. But one was allowed at least one catastrophe in life without losing face.

The fact that Phoebe's life had been one big catastrophe was something she preferred to ignore. Although she had lost a husband and her right to the family fortune in one fell swoop, dear Sedgely's accident was not her fault. Neither was his family's refusal to acknowledge her or their grandson once Sedgely was dead.

No, all in all, Phoebe thought as she gazed at the clumsy maypole, she could consider herself fortunate in her undertakings. The interjection of a divine hand, no doubt. There was, after all, a lot to be said for being the mother of a vicar.

Hearing voices, she straightened the very large brim of her hat and brushed invisible specks from the skirt of her gray silk gown. She was extremely proud of this gown. It had been purchased from a small but exclusive boutique on

Oxford Street, and while not exactly a Worth gown, it was a close facsimile of one.

Her hat had been especially trimmed to complement the gown, with white ostrich feathers and gray and blue chrysanthemums to match the embroidery on the long, graceful skirt. Phoebe might have seen better days financially, but that didn't mean she had to let appearances suffer.

The group of chattering young women rounded the corner of the church and came to a halt. Voices died away one by one as they each caught sight of the makeshift pole.

"It's only for rehearsal," Phoebe assured them. "When we do the May dance on the Downs, rest assured you shall have a proper maypole."

"My mum said there won't be a May dance this year because of that dreadful murder," a tubby young thing with big blue eyes announced.

There were lots of "oohs" and "ahs" as the girls huddled together in mock fright.

"Now, Marion, I am quite sure the police will have this matter cleared up by Friday," Phoebe said firmly. "Which is why I have arranged to have this pole set up here so that we can rehearse. It is essential that we know all the steps by heart if we are to give our usual spectacular performance. People expect it of us."

"Don't look very safe," one of the dancers announced, peering shortsightedly at the strips of sheet hanging mournfully from the bicycle wheel.

"It's perfectly secure," Phoebe said, beginning to feel just a teensy bit put out. She had gone to a great deal of trouble to arrange for this rehearsal, not to mention her spat with Algie. The vicar was violently opposed to having eight young women prancing about on the only decent stretch of grass in the entire grounds.

Phoebe had argued that it was the only spot on the grounds where they could not be observed from the street. She did not relish the idea of an audience previewing the performance. For one thing, the dancers were still unpolished.

For another, Phoebe liked the element of surprise when

presenting her masterpieces, which at times could be her undoing.

The girls stood chattering amongst themselves about the gruesome details of the murder, which seemed to have escalated into something quite horrific, having been embellished with each new rendition.

"They said her head was tucked underneath her arm, like the ghost who walks the Bloody Tower," Dora's strident voice proclaimed. "Her eyes were hanging out on her cheek."

"Ooh, my, it makes you feel quite ill," Belinda said with a moan. "I don't know as if I want to dance around that pole. It must be absolutely *saturated* in blood."

Shrieks of disgust followed this remark.

Phoebe clapped her hands. "Ladies, *please*. I can promise you there is no blood. Lady Sherbourne was strangled with one of the ribbons—"

More hysterical shrieks greeted this. Suspecting that the dancers were having a game with her, Phoebe decided to assert her authority. Crossing her arms over her bosom, she fixed them with a baleful stare. "The next person who makes that disgusting noise," she announced in a voice of doom, "will be replaced. Permanently."

Eight pairs of eyes regarded her in silence.

"Thank you." Phoebe stalked over to the pole. From behind her a voice muttered, "There ain't no one left to replace us. They all left for the flipping city."

A few hisses from her companions made it unnecessary for Phoebe to address that remark. "Now," she announced, holding up one of the strips. "I want each of you to take one of these and stand in a circle around the pole, as we did last week."

"What we going to do for music?" Dora asked as the girls bumped and nudged each other into position. "Lydia Willoughby isn't here to play the piano for us."

"Thank God for that," someone muttered. "She sounds bloody awful. I swear she plays with her fingers crossed."

"We'll have to sing," Phoebe said, hoping she wasn't asking for too much. "Now remember, ladies, Marion,

Isabelle, Dora, and Belinda go *out*side; the others go *in*side. You go in, out, in, out, weaving around each other until all the ribbons are wound around the pole. A chorus of 'Around the Mulberry Bush' will do very nicely. Then here we go, all-together on three . . . Ah one . . . two . . . three . . ."

The dancers stared in fascination as Phoebe opened her mouth to warble the opening bars, emitting a sound that even to her ears faintly resembled the foghorn on the lighthouse at Gallows Point.

"Bloody hell," someone said.

"Goodness gracious," an immature voice spoke in alarm from the porch. "Are you . . . ah . . . all right, Mother? Not having one of your . . . ah . . . turns, are you?"

A loud snort erupted from one of the dancers, triggering more giggles from the group.

Phoebe glared at the bespectacled man in the doorway. With the sun shining on his bald head and casting a sheen on the folds of his white cassock, he looked a little like a wayward angel.

"Maybe the vicar can play the organ for us?" someone piped up.

"Maybe we shall simply count out the steps," Phoebe said hurriedly. "Are we ready? Then let us begin—"

"I do hope you are not going to . . . ah . . . dance on my manicured lawn in those shoes?" Algie said, his voice rising in a whine.

"And I sincerely hope you are not going to stand there making asinine remarks," Phoebe snapped back before she could control herself.

Dora nudged her companion. "Oooh, listen to her cheek the vicar. Fancy cheeking the vicar."

"She's his mother," Marion said dryly. "If she can't cheek him, who can?"

"God," someone answered.

A howl of laughter rewarded that comment.

"Ladies, please!" Even Phoebe surprised herself with the wrath she'd managed to inject into her voice.

Eight mouths obediently snapped shut.

"Thank you." Phoebe grasped the brim of her hat, which

had become slightly dislodged with the force of her agitation. With a firm tug, she settled it more firmly on her head and took a deep breath.

"In the interest of peace and quiet"—once more she sent a lethal glance at Algie—"I shall ask you to please remove your shoes."

Ignoring the various squeals as bare toes made contact with the cool grass, Phoebe made sure to warn Algie with a final scowl.

In response, he folded his hands inside his long sleeves and waited with a pained expression on his round face.

"Now," Phoebe said, when order appeared to have been restored, "I will begin counting, and you will begin weaving. Remember, in and out. In and out. Are we ready? Then let's begin. Ah, one and two and three and four and—"

"Here, watch it! You've got your ribbon wrapped around my neck. I can't bloody breathe."

"It's your fault. You stuck your dirty big head in the way."

"Blimey, we'll all end up strangled like Lady Sherbourne at this rate."

"Here, stop shoving me, will you?"

"Ouch . . . that was my foot, you clumsy sod."

"Ladies, ladies!" Phoebe screamed. "I said around, not through! In and out, remember? Now do it again. One and two and three . . ."

Taken by surprise, the dancers leaped to obey. Unfortunately Dora went out when she should have gone in. She crashed headlong into Marion, who tripped over Isabelle's feet.

In slow motion, like a whale sinking into the sea, Marion subsided against the pole. It wobbled precariously back and forth, then in a majestic arc it sent the bicycle wheel hurtling down, straight at a stained-glass window.

Algie's agonized shriek mingled with the splintering of glass as multicolored sparks showered down onto the closely cropped grass in front of him.

For once not one of the awestruck dancers dared to utter a single comment.

*   *   *

Cecily stood at the wall of the Roof Garden, from where she could see the entire length of the Esplanade. The sun had begun to sink in the sky, sending the shadows of slanted roofs across the Esplanade almost to the railings.

This was the quiet hour before dinner. Most of the guests would be in their suites, changing into elegant gowns and evening dress for the sumptuous meal prepared for them by Michel.

This had been one of the few private interludes Cecily had been able to share with James during the height of the summer Season. She could never stand at that wall, with the sea breeze disturbing her tightly wound chignon, breathing in the fragrance of roses from the bushes planted in tubs all around her, without thinking of those special moments with the husband she had adored.

She had another reason to be there this evening, however. Sylvester had still not returned to the hotel. Cecily was determined to have a word with him, preferably while he was alone, which was the reason she had chosen that particular spot to sit in wait for him.

No matter from which direction he came, she would be able to see him approach the hotel. Unless he came through the stables, and she could be fairly certain that he wouldn't do so, since he hadn't taken out a horse. She had made sure of that.

So all Cecily had to do was wait until she saw him and waylay him on the steps outside the hotel, where she could have a private word with him.

She watched a seagull swoop low over the sea, then dip into the sparkling water before soaring to the sky once more, this time with something in its beak. She followed its flight across the cool, green Downs until it had disappeared.

As a child she had often wished she could fly. How wonderful it must be to glide effortlessly wherever one wished to go, without worrying about following roads or climbing stiles to cross fields. Much more territory could be discovered if one had the ease of flight to travel across countryside as yet untouched by the creeping hands of modernization.

The distant roar of a motorcar seemed to echo her thoughts. Even with the speed those machines could go, twelve miles an hour or better, they were still confined to the whim of the road upon which they traveled. And motorcars couldn't traverse stiles. There were still advantages to riding a horse.

Cecily dropped her gaze back to the Esplanade, her pulse quickening as she spied the tall figure striding toward the hotel from the direction of town. Sylvester had returned. Now was her opportunity to talk to him.

Heading for the narrow doorway that would take her to the main staircase, Cecily hoped she could meet him before he entered the hotel. She had a feeling that he might not care for the questions she had to put to him, and her task would be more easily accomplished if they could be assured of not being overheard.

She arrived, breathless and panting, at the base of the stairs a few minutes later. The lobby was empty, as was to be expected at this time of the day.

Cecily hurried across the lobby and through the doors, out onto the steps, where the breeze felt much cooler than it had in the shelter of the Roof Garden.

Not a moment too soon, she thought, as she saw Sylvester reach the bottom step and begin to climb toward her.

He seemed startled when she called out a greeting, as if disturbed in some deep thought. He paused in front of her, his blue eyes questioning. "Has something happened?" he asked abruptly.

Cecily shook her head. "Nothing more than has already happened," she said, noting his taut features and pinched mouth. "I wanted to offer my condolences on the tragedy. I know how devastated the entire family has been over the loss of Lady Sherbourne."

"Yes, yes. My poor brother . . ." Sylvester shook his head, as if words failed him.

"Speaking of your brother," Cecily said, "I am quite worried about him. I do wonder if this dreadful incident hasn't disturbed him to the point of derangement. A severe shock can do that to a person, so I understand."

Sylvester laid one hand against the wall, as if to steady himself. "What leads you to believe such a thing, Mrs. Sinclair?"

"Well, I talked to your wife. Lady Deirdre told me that you had spent the afternoon of Lady Sherbourne's disappearance in Lord Sherbourne's suite, going over accounts of the estate. Lord Sherbourne, however, is insisting he was alone that afternoon. I wonder if perhaps his memory is playing tricks with him."

She watched a muscle twitch in Sylvester's lean cheek. His eyes seemed to harden as he stared at her, and his voice was quite cool when he spoke. "His memory is not tricking him, Mrs. Sinclair, I can assure you. My brother was alone in his suite that afternoon and evening."

"Oh?" Cecily said, trying to sound innocent rather than nosy. "How strange. I wonder why Lady Deirdre seemed to be under the impression—"

"She was under the impression I was with him," Sylvester said evenly, "because that is what I told her."

Cecily met his stark gaze squarely. "I see," she said in a tone that suggested she didn't see at all.

Sylvester continued to stare at her for a moment or two, which she endured without flinching. Then he said quietly, "Mrs. Sinclair, I would greatly appreciate it if you did not inform my wife of what has just passed between us."

"I do not pass on gossip of any kind, Lord Boscombe. Your secret is safe with me."

He nodded, started to take his leave, then appeared to think better about it. "It is not too serious a matter," he said, once more fixing her with his intent gaze. "More of an embarrassment, to be honest. I happened to take a fancy to one of the . . . er . . . younger guests at this establishment. I followed her down onto the beach and spent a delightful hour or two talking with her. In full view of anyone who cared to pass by, I might add. All quite innocent, I assure you."

"Of course," Cecily murmured.

For the first time his stare faltered, and he looked past her to where the shadows now stretched across the sand. "My wife, however, is inclined to be a trifle possessive," he said, passing his beautifully manicured fingers across his forehead. "She would not understand the situation as well as a lady of your intelligence would do."

Cecily would have felt inclined to smile at his attempt to flatter her had she not been so certain that Sylvester was not speaking the truth. It was quite apparent that the youngest Boscombe brother was most disturbed about something. Something more than simply mourning for his dead sister-in-law. And Cecily would have given a great deal to know exactly what it was that had him so overwrought.

CHAPTER
❊ 11 ❊

"There are times, Baxter," Cecily said, "when I really do wonder what this world is coming to." She leaned back in her chair at the head of the library table and gazed upon the portrait of her late husband. "James would turn in his grave if he could see half of what is happening in Badgers End these days."

"He would indeed, madam." Baxter stood with his back to the door, hands clasped behind him in his usual posture. "In my opinion it is this constant scramble toward modernization that is the cause of the problems. Newfangled machines are being invented every day to do the work that men and women have done for centuries. I have heard that in America some of the better hotels now have a machine that can wash dishes. They even have a machine that can suck the dust from carpets into a bag. Quite amazing when you think about it."

Cecily smiled. "Oh, what I would give to own machines like that. Think how much easier life in this hotel would be if one didn't have to worry about beating the carpets or washing the dishes."

Baxter gave her one of his impassive looks. "Consider, if you will, what would happen to those people you employ to take care of such duties."

"Well, it's true, we wouldn't need quite so many people, but that would save us money, would it not?"

His eyes glinted at her. "Does the acquisition of wealth mean more to you than people?"

His remarks were beginning to pain her. Frowning, she said a trifle sharply, "Of course not, Baxter, you know better than that. I merely meant . . ." What had she meant?

"Precisely, madam. As is only natural, you would wish to take advantage of the benefits of modern machines. Otherwise why go to all the trouble of inventing them? Am I correct?"

She stared at him in frustration. Knowing him as well as she did, she knew he was leading up to something. Baxter always did take forever to come to the point. She had an uncomfortable feeling that this time his opinion would be a criticism of her values.

"I really don't see what is wrong with that," she protested. "After all, we must move with the times. Surely it isn't a crime to enjoy improvements in one's lifestyle?"

"I agree. As long as it isn't at the expense of others."

"Sometimes we cannot control the circumstances of others."

"Also agreed. All I am suggesting is that as more and more of these machines take the place of workers, there will be fewer jobs for the labor force. People will lose their livelihood and be forced to turn to other means in order to survive. Some of them will almost certainly turn to crime."

Cecily sighed. "You paint a dismal picture of the future, Baxter. I hope you are wrong in your estimation. There has to be some benefit derived from all the miserable suffering man has endured over the ages in order to better his living conditions."

"There will always be people who take advantage of their strength over the weak. I am afraid that as the world invents bigger and better machines, some of those people will harness the technology to find more powerful ways to destroy their enemies. Already the power of explosives is increasing at an alarming rate."

Uncomfortable with the direction of their conversation, Cecily said in a pained voice, "I really can't see what that has to do with machines that do housework."

"It is when people have too much time on their hands that they get into mischief."

Cecily's mind winged back to Sylvester Boscombe. There was a man with plenty of time on his hands. What kind of mischief had he indulged in that fateful afternoon when Lady Sherbourne had died?

"Baxter?" She looked up at him with a winning smile. "I would dearly love a cigar."

She watched his eyebrows lift and prepared herself for his lecture. At least she had successfully changed the subject.

He was about to speak when a light tap at the door interrupted him. Ethel stepped in, bobbing a curtsy.

"Sorry to disturb you, mum, but Lord Sherbourne is asking to see you. He's waiting outside in the hallway."

Cecily nodded. "Show him in, Ethel."

"Yes, mum."

"You wish me to stay, madam?" Baxter asked as Ethel disappeared.

"That won't be necessary, thank you. I'm sure it's nothing too important." She gave him a meaningful look. "If you care to return after he leaves, however, there's a little matter of a cigar . . ."

He was prevented from answering her by Ethel's fortuitous reappearance.

"Lord Sherbourne," she announced, standing back to allow the gentleman to pass her. Then with another quick dip she left in a flurry of skirts.

With a parting glance in her direction, Baxter greeted Lord Sherbourne, then swiftly left them alone.

One look at His Lordship's face told Cecily he was most

displeased with her. Before she could say anything, he leaned his fingertips on the desk and said harshly, "It has come to my attention, madam, that you have been badgering my family about matters that are none of your business."

"I beg your pardon, Lord Sherbourne," Cecily answered, making an effort to keep her voice even, "but anything untoward that takes place in this hotel is my business."

"If you are referring to the death of my wife"—he paused, as if attempting to control his grief—"then I must point out that the incident happened outside of this hotel, and therefore out of your jurisdiction."

"That's as may be. As a result of what happened, however, certain elements of my business will suffer if this matter is not cleared up shortly. And since the principal characters in the situation are staying at my hotel, I am simply trying to discover what happened to your wife."

"That, I do believe, is a matter for the police to investigate."

She pursed her lips. "You surprise me, Lord Sherbourne. I should have thought you would be the first to wish this crime solved and the perpetrator apprehended."

He straightened, an angry flush suffusing his cheeks. "Madam, I assure you no one has a greater desire to see this madman caught and punished than I have. In fact, it will be only with the greatest of restraint that I shall refrain from destroying him myself."

"I'm happy to hear that," Cecily murmured.

"My family has suffered a terrible loss, however. The trauma of shock and grief has affected us all. To be hounded by an insatiable snoop with nothing better on her mind than to satisfy her morbid curiosity is an abhorrence we should not have to suffer at this time. Please, madam, do us the extreme favor of leaving us in peace."

Cecily rose, her scalp tingling with her resentment. "Lord Sherbourne. Unlike our less than enthusiastic police force in these parts, I am of the belief that the longer the period following a crime without an investigation taking place, the better is the chance that the culprit will escape detection. I am doing my best to save our local constabulary from that unfortunate humiliation."

"How very thoughtful of you, madam." Lord Sherbourne moved to the door, then paused. "I must insist, however, that you refrain from harassing my family. I want no more of your impertinent questions with regards to my wife's unfortunate demise. From now on, any discussion on the subject will be reserved for the police."

Snapping his heels together, he inclined his head, then left the room.

Cecily felt a most childish urge to stick out her tongue. Sinking back onto her chair, she frowned at James's portrait. "I wonder," she said softly, "just who was worried enough about my questions to complain to Lord Sherbourne? If I knew that, perhaps I would be a little closer to discovering the truth."

James's face smiled back at her in complete agreement.

"Three days in a row," Mrs. Chubb announced early the next morning, "is a bit much. It's still an hour before breakfast. I think this time we should go up and knock him up in time for him to come down and eat it."

"What?" Gertie lifted the tub off the stove with a loud grunt. "Strewth, I swear this bloody thing gets heavier every time I lift it."

"Captain Phillips." Mrs. Chubb glanced up at the clock on the mantelpiece. "I think we should wake him up and insist he come down for breakfast. Or have one taken up. The man has to be ill not to eat his meals in three days."

"Probably bleeding hung over," Gertie said. "You know what these bleeding sailors are like. I bet he's got a few blinking bottles of rum under his bed and is swigging them down one by one."

"He's never done anything like this before," Mrs. Chubb said, only half listening.

"Yeah? You don't know what that old geezer gets up to when you're not around. What with him and that daffy colonel . . ." She paused, a grin spreading over her face. "Know what he thinks now? He thinks he saw a flipping man on a horse, without a bleeding head. He reckons he was the one what done Lady Sherbourne in."

"Captain Phillips?" Mrs. Chubb said in astonishment. "How does he know anything? He's been in his room since the day of the murder."

Gertie shook her head so hard her cap slid sideways. Catching it with one hand, she shoved it back in place. "Nah, not him. That Colonel Fortescue, that's who. Ethel told me. She heard him blabbering that night, she did. Like a flipping baby, she said, his voice all high and funny like. Said it was a headless horseman what strangled Her Ladyship."

Mrs. Chubb clicked her tongue against her teeth. "The poor man. I often wonder what will become of him."

"Don't do too bleeding bad, does he?" Gertie said, plunging her hands into the hot soapy water. "Spends most of his time down here at the Pennyfoot. Makes you wonder what kind of home he's got, don't it?" She lifted her head. "Here, what if the colonel was the one what done the murder?"

"Gertie!" Mrs. Chubb waved a silver serving spoon at her. "You'd better watch your tongue, my girl. You know very well it was more likely one of the gypsies who did it. You and your quick tongue. You'd get a vicar hung, you would."

Gertie sighed. "Well, if you ask me, our vicar's just as bad an' all, with his silly voice and that prissy walk. Should have been a girl, he should. He bloody acts like one, that's for blinking sure."

"Gertie, that's enough! Now get upstairs and knock Captain Phillips up again. Tell him it's hotel rules he has to eat something. That will get him out of there."

"Ow, Mrs. Chubb, do I have to? My legs ache terrible, and me back, and me stomach feels like shit—"

"Gert-ay!"

The housemaid's mouth shut in a thin line.

Mrs. Chubb took a closer look at her. "Are you feeling all right?"

"No, I'm bleeding not."

To Mrs. Chubb's dismay, Gertie lifted her arms out of the water and howled into her apron.

Instantly contrite, the housekeeper hurried over and put an arm around the girl's trembling shoulders. "Here, here, ducks, don't let it get you down, then, there's a good girl. Come and sit down for a minute and tell me what's the matter."

Sniffing and snuffling, Gertie plopped down on a chair. "I'm bleeding pregnant, aren't I."

Stunned, Mrs. Chubb stared at Gertie's tear-stained face. "Pregnant? But that's wonderful! I thought that's what you wanted." A thought struck her, and she leaned closer. "It is all right, isn't it? I mean there's nothing? Wrong with the baby, is there?"

"Nah." Gertie sniffed and wiped her nose with the back of her hand.

"Blow your nose, dear," Mrs. Chubb murmured, then rolled her eyes at the ceiling when Gertie lifted a corner of her apron and trumpeted into it.

"Now," she said, when Gertie seemed to have calmed down a bit, "what's the matter, then?"

"I told Ian," Gertie said dismally.

"So what did he say?"

"He says he don't . . . want . . . it. . . ." Once more Gertie burst into loud sobs.

"Oh, my." Mrs. Chubb fanned her face with the spoon, then put it down carefully on the table. "Did he say why? I mean, he must have known . . ."

"That's what I told him." Gertie hiccupped and swiped at her nose again. "I told him if he didn't want a blinking baby, why did he want to do it all the time . . . you know what I mean? He said he couldn't help himself."

Mrs. Chubb scowled. "Men never can," she said darkly. "There are ways to . . . er . . . do it and not get pregnant. Not that I agree with it, of course. Not natural, I say. If God wanted us to have a choice whether or not we got pregnant, he'd have found a way to provide for it."

"Well, that don't bloody help me now, does it?" Gertie

gave her a fierce look. "And I ain't getting bloody rid of it, so there."

"Oh, heaven preserve us, I wouldn't let you do that, my girl, and you know it. I only helped you before because I knew you weren't pregnant that time. But if the doctor says you are . . ." She paused and peered into Gertie's face. "He did say you are, didn't he?"

Gertie nodded. "I thought Ian would be as pleased as punch, I did. After all, he's always having fun with the kids in the blinking village. But when I told him, he went bleeding bonkers. Said we couldn't afford it and that I'd have to give up work and just when we were getting the cottage the way we wanted it."

"How strange," Mrs. Chubb said, frowning.

Gertie looked up with a loud sniff. "What is?"

"Well, Ian was so dead set against you working before you got married."

"Yeah, well, that was before, weren't it. Changed his bleeding mind now, he has. Bit bloody late though, that's what I say."

"Well, I'm quite sure he'll come around." Mrs. Chubb bustled over to the stove and picked up the kettle. "Just don't you worry, you'll see. Bit of a shock, I reckon, coming out of the blue like that. Give him a day or two to get used to it, and he'll be fine."

"I bleeding hope so. Otherwise we'll be arguing for the rest of our bloody lives about it."

Mrs. Chubb filled the kettle and carried it back to the stove. "Well, I'm going to make you a nice hot cup of tea, and you'll feel better in no time. While you're drinking it, I'll go up myself and knock Captain Phillips up. He'll more likely come out of there for me than he would for you."

That got a smile out of the housemaid. "Bleeding kidding yourself, ain't yer?"

"Watch your tongue, my girl," Mrs. Chubb said, reaching into the cupboard for a teacup. But she couldn't help feeling pleased with herself for cheering the girl up.

She was still smiling about it as she climbed the stairs to the top landing. Poor Gertie. Things always seemed to be such a tragedy at that age. Just wait until Gertie had lived as long as she had. Then she'd know what life was really all about.

There were far worse things in the world than a husband's shock over the news of a baby. Look at poor Lady Sherbourne for instance. What a terrible way to end her life, and so young and pretty, too. Crying shame, it was. And the murderer not caught yet. One never knew where he might turn up next.

She reached the top step, holding her aching side. She didn't often climb the stairs now. Just once a week to see that the housemaids were doing their job. Her old bones couldn't take all that climbing up and down anymore. Sometimes it was all she could do to climb out of bed.

Walking along the hallway, she wondered if Captain Phillips had been in bed all this time. If so, he'd be as weak as a kitten by now, without food or drink. Twice she'd sent meals up to his room, only to have the maid come back down saying he didn't want anything.

Pausing in front of the door, she lifted her hand to knock. It seemed awfully quiet in there. After looking up and down the landing, she pressed her ear to the door. Not a dicky bird. Probably asleep. He'd probably be mad as a tormented bull to be woken up. It couldn't be helped, though. A man needed his nourishment to survive. And she wasn't about to let anyone die of starvation in her territory, thank you. She'd never hear the last of it.

Taking a deep breath, she rapped sharply on the door.

No answer. Nothing. Not even a moan.

She rapped again, louder this time. "Captain Phillips? I know you are in there. It's Mrs. Chubb, the housekeeper. I must insist that you eat something, Captain. We are responsible for you while you are in this hotel. Can I have something sent up here to your room?"

"Watcha want?" the captain said in his gravelly voice from inside the room.

"I want you to eat something, Captain. I can have Mr. Baxter bring some food up to your room. Perhaps you'd like me to fetch Dr. Prestwick to look at you?"

"Drop bleeding dead."

"Well!" Affronted, Mrs. Chubb glared at the closed door. "Captain Phillips," she said loudly. "I must insist—"

"Watchableeding want?"

Mrs. Chubb frowned. Something was not right here. Not right at all. She could almost feel it. Grasping the handle, she twisted it sharply back and forth, but the door remained defiantly closed.

Farther down the hallway another door opened, and a sleepy-looking head wearing a nightcap peered at her. "What the blue blazes is going on here?" a hoarse voice demanded.

"Sorry to disturb you, sir," Mrs. Chubb said quickly. "We seem to be having a problem with the gentleman in this room."

"No," the irate voice corrected, "you do not have a problem with the gentleman in that room. He has been remarkably quiet. The problem appears to be with you and your staff, screaming at the top of your lungs at an unearthly hour in the morning, loud enough to wake everybody up within a twelve-mile radius."

From inside the captain's room a gravelly voice said, "Drop bleeding dead."

"I'm sorry," Mrs. Chubb began again, then she snapped her mouth shut when a husky voice spoke from behind the angry guest. "Poopsie, darling? Come and warm me up, my sweet."

With a grunt of disgust the head withdrew and the door slammed shut.

Wincing, Mrs. Chubb turned around and headed for the stairs. Something was wrong all right. If the captain hadn't put in an appearance by dinnertime that evening, she would have to get Mr. Baxter to come up and open the door with his special keys. One way or another, she had to find out what was going on in that room.

CHAPTER

❖12❖

Phoebe sped up the steps of the Pennyfoot the next morning as fast as her long, tight skirt would allow. Enough was enough. She wasn't sure what Cecily could do about the situation, but she was at her wit's end. Either she got a rehearsal at the maypole on the Downs that very day, or there would be no May dance.

She flew into the foyer, nearly colliding with Colonel Fortescue, who was on his way out.

"'Pon my word, madam, we are in a hurry this morning, are we not?" the colonel said, standing back to allow her to pass.

Phoebe regarded the portly gentleman with a suspicious eye. One never knew in what kind of mood one would find him. Sometimes he could be quite pleasant. Other times he was most certainly insane.

"I say," the colonel said, blinking hard as he leaned toward her, "he's not after you, is he?"

Phoebe looked over her shoulder. "To whom are you referring, pray?"

"Why, that poor blighter who lost his head, of course. Been running around the cliffs at night, up to God knows what mischief. Dashed odd that, what? What?"

"Very," Phoebe said solemnly. It always helped to humor the silly man when he was like this.

"Yes, well." He looked left, then right, then lifted a finger and laid it against his luxurious white mustache. "It's the gypsies," he whispered, "going around cutting off people's heads."

"Is it really?" Phoebe whispered back. "How absolutely ghastly."

"Quite, quite." He lowered his hand and boomed out in his usual loud voice, "Well, only two more days until May Day. All the girlies in their pretty frocks cavorting around the maypole. Spiffing sight, what?"

Reminded of the reason she was there, Phoebe nodded vigorously. "Oh, absolutely, Colonel. We can't disappoint the local gentry, now can we? You know how Lord Withersgill always enjoys the May Day festivities."

"Oh, yes, as do we all, m'dear, as do we all. Let's just hope there won't be any more dead bodies hanging on the dratted thing. That would certainly put a damper on things, what?"

Phoebe's smile froze. "Yes, well, if you will excuse me, Colonel, I really do have to be getting along."

"Oh, righto, old bean. Right ho." He put up a hand to doff his hat, realized he wasn't wearing one, and looked vaguely around as if expecting it to materialize in front of him. "Must have left it in the room," he muttered. "Getting blasted absentminded. That won't do, oh, dear me no . . ." So saying, he ambled back toward the stairs, shaking his head and muttering to himself.

Phoebe waited until he had turned the first bend before venturing down the hallway in search of Cecily.

She found her in the dining room, discussing the table settings with one of the maids.

"I'll be very happy when Madeline returns from London," Cecily said after sending the maid scurrying off to obey her orders. "She always takes care of these details so well. No one handles flowers the way Madeline does."

"Well, perhaps it is just as well she isn't here." Phoebe cast a practiced eye around the tables. "What with all this talk about gypsies running amok, someone might take it into his head to accuse her of something. You know how suspicious the villagers are of anyone who is different."

"It doesn't stop them from buying Madeline's potions when they have a problem to take care of," Cecily said tartly. "They certainly trust her then."

"That's as may be. But anyone who goes around talking about spirits and ghosts, and who acts the way Madeline does sometimes, is bound to get an unfavorable reputation."

Cecily looked as if she might argue, then apparently changed her mind. "Well," she said mildly, "I'm sure you didn't come here to discuss Madeline's reputation. Is there something I can do for you?"

Phoebe sighed. "I don't know if you can, my dear. I have exhausted my patience, I can tell you. I admire the constable greatly, but sometimes he can be extraordinarily obtuse."

"P. C. Northcott takes his job very seriously," Cecily said, leaning across a table to pinch off a dead leaf from the display of delphiniums in the delicate china vase.

"Albeit too seriously at times." Phoebe chose a chair and flounced down on it. "He absolutely refuses to give me permission to use the maypole for a rehearsal. I cannot imagine what he expects the inspector to find that hasn't already been discovered. By the time that idiot has finished tramping around with his notebook in one hand and a magnifying glass in the other, he'll do far more damage in his hobnail boots than a hundred dancers in pumps could possibly manage."

"I imagine he has certain regulations that have to be observed."

Phoebe eyed the delphiniums with distaste. She never did

like the blooms and could have sworn she'd heard some-where that they were poisonous. "Well, all I can say is that his regulations will very likely sabotage any hopes of providing a presentable performance of the May dance. I can't believe that those silly girls could have forgotten how to do it since last year. Of course, three of them weren't in the group last year, but still—"

"Phoebe, I am quite sure that the constable must have finished with his investigation by now. I would suggest you simply go on up there this morning and have your rehearsal. By the time the constable discovers what you have done, it will be too late to do anything about it."

"Well, I don't know that I want to upset a policeman—"

"I'll take full responsibility," Cecily said firmly. "Of course, there is always the possibility that the entire May Day festivities will be canceled anyway. But if not, you, at least, will be prepared."

Phoebe rose, fluttering her lace handkerchief in front of her face. "I shall indeed. Though heaven knows if my dancers will be." She tucked the handkerchief into her sleeve. "Thank you, Cecily, you have taken a great load off my mind. I must hurry now and get a message to all the dancers to meet me on the Downs."

She turned to go, then looked back. "I don't suppose you would have time for a spot of lunch with me at Dolly's afterward? I'll be happy to treat, a small thanks for your help."

Cecily considered the invitation for a moment. "That sounds like a wonderful idea. It would be good to get out of the hotel for a short while. Perhaps a breath of fresh air will shake the cobwebs loose. Yes, I'd like that very much."

"Excellent. Let us say at half past twelve? That's if I can round everyone up in time to get through a rehearsal."

"I could send Samuel or Ian out with the message if that would help."

Phoebe clasped her hands together in gratitude. "Oh, Cecily, you are an absolute angel. That would be wonderful indeed. It would save me so much time."

"Very well. You'll find one of them out in the stables. Just tell them where you want them to go, and tell them they have my permission."

"I will. And thank you so much. I will see you later, then." Phoebe lifted her hand in farewell and pranced out the door.

Feeling heady with relief, she hurried along the passage-way, her mind working on the problem of gathering the dancers together for an immediate rehearsal. Two of them worked up at Lord Withersgill's mansion, while the rest worked on the various farms. It would take at least an hour to get word to them all, another hour for the rehearsal. She would have to speed things up.

If only she had learned to ride during her brief marriage to dear Sedgely. If only Algie could ride. Ridiculous thought, of course. Algie had trouble standing on a chair. He'd never survive the trauma of sitting astride a horse. Ever since his father's death, he'd been terrified of horses.

Bursting out through the front doors, Phoebe pulled up short as she came face-to-face with a waif in a raggedy dress and the most ridiculous maroon velvet hat she'd ever seen. Utterly shapeless, it was, and hopelessly outdated.

The poor woman looked as if a good meal would do her good. Phoebe's heart bumped uncomfortably when it oc-curred to her she could be a gypsy. If it wasn't for the fact that she would be accompanied on the Downs by eight fairly hefty dancers, Phoebe would not have gone within a hundred miles of the place. "Excuse me," the woman said, causing Phoebe's pulse to leap in apprehension. She hoped fervently she wouldn't have to buy some lavender or clothes pegs. She had no need for either, but she couldn't risk a curse.

She would have loved to ignore the woman and simply brush past her. But that would never do. Once her back was turned, the gypsy would almost certainly place a curse on her. She once knew a woman who couldn't stop shaking. Couldn't even hold a teacup in her hand without slopping the contents all over her. Everyone knew the poor thing had been cursed by a gypsy.

"Yes?" she said nervously, switching her gaze to the

street beyond in the hopes of seeing someone else close enough to assist her should she need it.

The Esplanade, however, was deserted. It was too early for most of the gentry to be out and about.

"I'm looking for someone by the name of Robert Johnson," the woman said, peering earnestly up at her.

Phoebe stared into the large brown eyes. They didn't look evil. In fact, they looked rather pathetic. "I'm very sorry," she said politely, "but I have never heard of the gentleman. Perhaps someone in the hotel can help you."

The young woman shook her head. "I tried. No one will tell me anything."

"I'm sure they would if they could," Phoebe assured her. "They are most helpful."

"He works here," the woman said, giving her a mournful look. "But I think he's working under another name."

"Ah, I see," Phoebe said, not seeing at all. "Well, I'm so sorry I couldn't be of any help to you."

To her extreme dismay, the young woman barred her way. "He's about this tall, twenty-eight years old, light brown wavy hair, and blue eyes. He has a cheeky smile and is always joking with people."

"Oh," Phoebe said, carelessly waving her hand. "That sounds like Ian Rossiter."

The girl's eyes gleamed with sudden fire. "Ian who?"

"Rossiter. He's the stable manager. As a matter of fact, I am going there now if you'd care to come with me. Then you can see for yourself if he's the right person."

"Thank you," the woman said in a fierce manner. "Thanks ever so."

"Don't mention it. My pleasure, I'm sure." Phoebe was surprised by this intense gratitude for such a simple gesture. She led the way down the steps and around the corner of the hotel, wondering if perhaps she hadn't made a mistake in inviting the strange young woman along.

She could almost feel the tension radiating off the frail body as they passed through the gate together. "Of course, I don't suppose for one minute it is the man you are looking for," she said, beginning to feel a little nervous about this whole thing. "After all, I cannot imagine for the life of me why Ian would use a different name."

"Well, we'll find out, won't we?" her companion muttered with not a trace of her former respect.

Phoebe stopped short, certain now she'd made a grave error. This young woman could be a gypsy after all, out to wreak some sort of havoc on Ian Rossiter's life for some obscure reason. "On second thought," she said firmly, "Ian couldn't possibly be the man you are looking for. He's much taller, and his hair isn't really light brown, and—"

All at once she was talking to thin air. The woman had darted past her and was running toward the stable, her threadbare skirt flapping around her ankles.

Picking her way across the yard, one hand hitching her skirt, the other pinching her nostrils closed, Phoebe followed as fast as she could.

She saw the woman disappear inside the stables. Throwing caution to the wind, Phoebe increased her pace to catch her up. When she reached the stable doors, which stood open, she saw the young woman walking slowly down the length of the stalls to where a figure stood harnessing a restless horse.

Phoebe could see Ian's face quite clearly when he looked up and noticed the woman approaching him. Phoebe could only describe his expression afterward as akin to someone observing a major disaster.

Although the woman spoke quietly, Phoebe heard every word. "Hello, Robert," she said. "I've found you at last."

"I have to admit, Baxter," Cecily said as she watched him water the rosebushes in the Roof Garden, "it is worth the time and trouble to tend to the bushes. They are quite remarkable roses."

"They are indeed, madam."

"And I know John appreciates your taking care of them for him. His legs just won't allow him to climb all the way up here, I'm afraid."

"My pleasure, madam." He gave her a quick glance out of

the corner of his eye. "You seem preoccupied. I trust there have been no further developments in the murder case?"

Cecily sighed. "I am at a loss as to how to proceed with this investigation. I feel that Sylvester was not being entirely truthful when he gave me an explanation of where he was that afternoon. Yet I can hardly accuse him of lying. And I have no way of proving what is, after all, merely conjecture."

Baxter dipped the large watering can into the rain barrel to refill it. "I must confess, madam, I am relieved to hear you say that. Perhaps now you will let the police take care of the matter."

"And then it will be much too late to save the May Day festivities," Cecily said with a sigh. "The Women's Guild needs an entire day to set up the fête, as does Mr. Gordon for his Punch-and-Judy show. Phoebe is having trouble with the dancers, and the flowers have to be picked a day in advance for the Flower Show. The inspector is not due back until the weekend. Unless we get this investigation over with by tomorrow morning at the latest, our May Day is doomed."

Baxter dribbled water over one of the gaily painted tubs. They were actually beer barrels cut in half, and had been decorated by James's loving hand. Cecily could still remember the trouble Mrs. Chubb had had getting the paint splatters out of his clothes.

"On the contrary, madam," Baxter said, disturbing her memories. "I neglected to inform you earlier. Inspector Cranshaw returned to Wellercombe late last night. He is most likely at this moment carrying out his investigation."

Taken by surprise, Cecily frowned at him. "You neglected to tell me?"

"My apologies, madam. I simply forgot."

"That isn't like you, Baxter."

"No, madam."

"Well, at least now we shall perhaps see a swift solution to the murder," Cecily said without too much conviction. "I wish I had been privy to whatever Stan Northcott had been able to uncover at the murder scene. With that information I might have been able to solve this before now." She brushed the dust from her skirt. "I had best get back to my suite. I daresay the inspector will be here shortly to question the family."

Baxter cleared his throat. "From what I have been able to ascertain, the inspector is focusing his investigation on the gypsy encampment. Ian heard the news in the George and Dragon last night."

"The gypsies." Cecily made a small sound of disgust. "You see, I knew this would happen if it were left to P.C. Northcott. He was reluctant to question the Boscombes because of their standing, and now he's convinced the inspector the gypsies are to blame."

"We can't be certain that they are not, madam," Baxter reminded her gently. "According to Ian, the theory is that Lord Sherbourne quarreled with his wife, and she left on her own to relieve her anger by walking on the Downs. She was attacked by someone, and since she was in an area that has been recognized as being inhabited by lawbreakers, I would think it prudent of the inspector to direct his inquiries in that direction."

"I do not believe for one minute the gypsies are involved in this," Cecily said, feeling more frustrated by the second. "There are certain members of the family who have lied to me when questioned, and to me that suggests they have something to hide. Cranshaw is wasting valuable time harassing a group of people simply because they have a questionable reputation."

"I must remind you, madam, that you have no knowledge of the evidence Northcott may have uncovered. He could have discovered something that incriminates a member of the gypsies."

"Maybe so," Cecily said grimly. "But I, for one, would very much like to know why at least two members of the Boscombe family found it so necessary to lie about their whereabouts. I intend to find out."

"I do wish you would leave it in the hands of the police," Baxter said, looking a little desperate. "You mentioned yourself that Lord Sherbourne is displeased with you for questioning his family."

"I do not have time to leave it in the hands of the police if they insist on going on a wild-goose chase. For the past four hundred years the village of Badgers End has celebrated May Day. I am determined that this year shall be no exception."

She swung around and headed for the door. "Please finish watering the roses for me, Baxter. I have something I must do."

"Very well, madam."

She could tell by his huffy tone he was displeased with her. That was unfortunate, but she could not pay heed to him now. Time was running out, and if the festivities for May Day were going to take place, something had to be done. The sooner the better.

CHAPTER

❋13❋

From her vantage point in the Roof Garden, Cecily had seen Lady Grace walking unescorted in the gardens. Now, hurrying down the outside steps of the hotel, Cecily was intent on making the most of this opportunity.

She made for the Rose Garden, but this time the quiet corner was deserted. A small group of guests milled around the croquet lawns, and in the distance Cecily could hear the steady *thwack* of a tennis racket from the grass court. Lady Grace, however, was not an observer of either game.

Cecily was about to give up when she spied the woman walking beneath the row of hazelnut trees alongside the rock pool. She seemed absorbed in the grasses at her feet and didn't look up until Cecily was almost upon her.

Although she seemed startled at first, she recovered quickly and gave Cecily a warm smile. "How nice to see you out here, Mrs. Sinclair, on this lovely day. You are always so busy, I don't imagine you have much time to enjoy these lovely surroundings."

"I must confess you are quite right," Cecily said, returning the smile. "The opportunity is all the more pleasurable when it arises."

"Yes, indeed." Grace let her gaze wander across the lawns. "You are fortunate to have such a competent gardener to take care of everything for you. Good service is so difficult to find nowadays, even in the city. I would think it would be almost impossible in this isolated area of the coast."

"It is becoming increasingly difficult," Cecily assured her. "With so many of our young people leaving the villages and farms to find a new life in the cities, we will soon have no one to replace the older generation. I often wonder what would happen to the grounds of the Pennyfoot if John could no longer take care of them."

"He does remarkably well, considering he handles the entire estate on his own." Grace gave her another of her gracious smiles. "You must beware, Mrs. Sinclair, for I would dearly love to steal him from you."

Cecily laughed. "I don't think John would be happy in the city. He has lived here all his life and is as much a part of this village as are the trees and plants he loves so much."

Grace sighed. "More's the pity."

"He would be most pleased to hear of your compliments, if I may pass them on?"

Grace looked at her blankly for several seconds, as if she didn't understand. Then she said quickly, "Oh, by all means. He is certainly deserving of my admiration for his work."

"Thank you." Cecily paused, then added, "He was most appreciative of the fact you admired his roses so much. He mentioned that you had spent the entire afternoon gazing at them. I do believe that was the day your sister-in-law was murdered?"

Grace's eyelashes flickered, but she didn't answer.

"The day you told your husband you had taken to your bed with a wretched headache all afternoon," Cecily prompted gently.

Grace averted her gaze to her feet, her face showing signs

of distress. Then she looked up again. "John is correct," she said quietly. "I was in the Rose Garden. I had arranged to meet Lady Sherbourne there. I had a matter of the utmost importance to discuss with her. I waited for the entire afternoon, but she didn't arrive, of course. It wasn't until the next morning that I learned the reason for her failure to meet me."

Cecily frowned. "I don't understand why you wished to keep that a secret from your husband."

"I would appreciate it, Mrs. Sinclair, if you would not mention it to him or to anyone else. I prefer not to discuss the matter with anyone. Since my poor sister-in-law is now deceased, I see no reason to disclose a matter that could be of great embarrassment to certain members of the family."

"Milady, while I certainly respect your desire to protect your privacy, I must remind you that Lady Sherbourne was brutally murdered. The police will no doubt wish to question me, particularly about events that transpired that afternoon. Under the circumstances, I would be forced to tell them what I know. I think you must be prepared to disclose the reason you wished to meet with Lady Sherbourne, if only to remove suspicion from yourself."

Lady Grace lifted a hand to her throat. "You certainly don't think they will suspect me of being a cold-blooded murderer? Why, that's preposterous. I can assure you my intentions were perfectly innocent. I posed no threat to my sister-in-law."

"Perhaps if you were to tell me . . ." Cecily let her voice trail off, leaving the rest of the sentence to insinuation.

After a moment Grace said with a great deal of reluctance, "I am afraid, Mrs. Sinclair, that my husband had formed an unfortunate . . . attachment to Lady Sherbourne. He was quite infatuated with her, in fact. He had pursued her for a long time."

Noting the pain on the woman's rather plain face, Cecily felt sorry for her. She had been no match for Lady Sherbourne's classic beauty. While she searched for something sympathetic to say, Grace continued.

"Barbara had no interest in my husband, of course. Why

should she with a man like Radley for a husband? He was everything she could possibly want in a man. But Barbara enjoyed the kind of attention my husband was willing to lavish on her. She thrived on it." Grace's voice sounded remarkably prosaic, considering the content of her conversation. "She encouraged Arthur, while holding him at bay when he became too ardent, thus sending him almost insane with his frustration."

"I'm sorry," Cecily said quietly. "That must have been as traumatic for you as it was for your husband."

"Yes, it was." Grace's soft eyes pleaded with her. "But you must believe me, Mrs. Sinclair. I wished my sister-in-law no harm. I love my husband very much. I was convinced that if Barbara simply told him that she wasn't interested in his overtures, he would have overcome his infatuation in time, and perhaps rekindled his interest in me."

She lifted her hands in a helpless gesture and let them fall. "That is the reason for my meeting with Barbara. I intended to beg her, on my knees if necessary, to end my husband's misery. That is all."

"And now she is no longer a complication for you."

Grace shook her head. "Mrs. Sinclair, believe me when I say that I am very sad that my sister-in-law has met with this dreadful end. I would not have wished that on her. But now that she has gone, I see no reason to bring up this weakness of my husband's. I am hoping that we can find our way back to the affection we once shared."

Cecily wished with all her heart she could give her the assurance she sought. "I hope that you can, Lady Grace. While I can make no promises, I will endeavor to keep this confidence from public knowledge. You must understand that if I am forced to disclose the matter during the investigation, I shall have no choice but to comply."

Tight-lipped, Grace nodded. "I understand."

After bidding her farewell, Cecily retraced her steps back to the hotel, her brow creased in thought. So engrossed was she that she failed to see Baxter until he halted in front of her in the lobby, his voice showing a trace of concern.

"Madam? There is a problem?"

She looked up at him, smiling at his anxious frown. "I'm not sure, Baxter. Perhaps we should go to the library, and I'll tell you what I have heard."

He stood back to let her precede him down the hallway, his expression saying clearly that he anticipated as much.

Once inside the peaceful confines of the library, Cecily took her seat at the head of the table. With Baxter standing patiently by the door, his intent gaze on her face, she related everything that Grace had told her.

"I trust you won't repeat any of this to anyone," she said when she reached the end. "I gave my word to milady that I would not disclose her confidence unless forced to by the constabulary."

"I shall not tattle, madam," Baxter said a little stiffly.

"The thing that most concerns me," Cecily said, her gaze traveling to the portrait on the wall, "is not the matter of Lady Grace's innocence. After all, since John saw her in the Rose Garden the entire afternoon, she could hardly have been on the Downs with Lady Sherbourne."

"Quite."

"But she was also alone. Arthur was not with her. He mentioned that he had spent the afternoon walking into town and had called in at Dolly's Tea Shop for refreshments. I am going there myself this lunchtime. It will give me an excellent opportunity to verify his story."

"You suspect Arthur Boscombe of murdering his sister-in-law?" Baxter said in astonishment.

Cecily looked at him. "I don't know what I suspect right at this moment, Baxter. But I do think it's possible that Arthur, frustrated and thwarted in his attempts to win the object of his affections, perhaps driven to uncontrollable anger by the rejection of the woman he adored, could have reached the point where vengeance was uppermost in his mind. The worm turned, so to speak."

"That would be an exceedingly dramatic turnabout for someone with such a placid personality," Baxter said, sounding skeptical.

"Perhaps." Cecily's gaze returned to her husband's portrait. "But as all of us well know, the most tranquil of men have killed for one reason or another. And I can assure you, if Arthur Boscombe murdered his brother's wife, I shall make it my business to know about it before too long."

"And that," Baxter said solemnly, "is what terrifies me most of all."

"Ian isn't here, mum," Samuel said when Cecily confronted him in the stables later. "He went home more than two hours ago."

"Home? Is he not well?"

Samuel shrugged. "I don't know, not to be sure. He didn't look all that good. He had some woman with him, and she didn't look much better. All skinny and scrawny she was, like a plucked chicken. Ian asked me to take Mrs. Carter-Holmes into town, and then he left with the woman to go home."

"A woman?" She had a dreadful feeling she knew to which woman Samuel referred. "What did this woman look like?"

Her anxiety deepened as she listened to Samuel's description. It was the same woman she'd seen loitering around the stable door the day before. "Did he seem to know her?" she asked the footman.

"Not only did he look like he knew her, he seemed scared to death of her." Samuel shook his head. "Makes me wonder if she weren't one of those gypsies or something. I never seen Ian look like that. I didn't think he was afraid of anything."

Cecily sighed. It certainly sounded as if Ian was in some kind of trouble. Right now, however, she had an appointment to keep and couldn't waste any more time on useless conjectures. She would have to wait until she saw Ian in order to question him. She would deal with it then, she decided.

After instructing Samuel to take her to Dolly's Tea Shop in the High Street, she climbed into the trap and settled back to enjoy the ride.

The good weather looked as if it would hold for a few

more days at least, though living on the brink of the Channel, one never knew when a sudden squall would surprise everyone.

The warmth of the sun felt wonderful as it penetrated her thin muslin sleeves. It was so nice to be able to drive with the hood down and feel the sea air filling her lungs. It had been a cold winter and a late spring. The summer months were so short as it was, and one had to make the most of the good weather while the opportunity was there.

It would seem as if other people had the same idea, as the Esplanade seemed unusually busy for a week day out of Season. Cecily enjoyed watching the people stroll along the railings or pause to peer into the leaded bay windows of the little shops.

The trap had almost reached the High Street when she spied a familiar figure. Dr. Prestwick, his black bag grasped firmly in one hand, stood at the curb waiting to cross as Cecily approached.

He lifted his hand to touch his hat, his warm smile lighting up his face. "How pleasant to see you, Cecily," he called out as they passed.

"Samuel, pull up, please," Cecily said on impulse. "I wish to have a word with the doctor."

Samuel obediently hauled on the reins, bringing the snorting chestnut to a standstill. Cecily swiveled in her seat, in time to see the doctor striding toward her.

"You are not ill, I trust?" he said as he reached her.

His blue eyes twinkled at her when she shook her head. "I am perfectly healthy, thank you, Doctor."

"I am happy to hear it. Though I do wish we had more occasion to meet. I have been meaning to pay you a visit at the hotel but haven't had the time, as yet."

Cecily smiled down at him, reflecting that Baxter wouldn't be too pleased to see him. Baxter always displayed the most peculiar attitude whenever she and the doctor visited together.

"Being the only doctor in the village, you must have your hands full," she said, adding innocently, "Then, of course, you have the police work to take care of as well."

Dr. Prestwick wagged a warning finger at her. "Now, now, Cecily, you know I am not at liberty to discuss police business."

Cecily laughed. "I doubt you could tell me anything I don't already know. Do the police really think the gypsies are responsible for that dreadful murder?"

"They do indeed." His handsome face regarded her, and she could tell he was not in total agreement with that revelation.

"And what do you think?" she asked, attempting to sound as if she attached no real importance to his answer.

The doctor glanced up at Samuel, who sat stiff-backed on the driver's seat. Then he leaned closer, his arm resting on the side of the trap. "I can tell you one thing," he said softly. "She did not attempt to fight very hard to save her skin. Her clothes were not ripped, nor did I find any bruises, except for the one around her throat."

"You are saying she knew her attacker," Cecily said, feeling inordinately pleased with herself.

The doctor placed a finger over his lips, as if denying her observation. "Lady Sherbourne was a beautiful, wealthy woman," he said. "Some women who have everything can in time become bored. I believe it is possible she could have become enamored of a dashing, virile gypsy, who appeared so different from anyone she had known before, so exciting and yet so very dangerous."

"Who killed her in a mad, passionate frenzy of jealousy because she would not run away with him, preferring to return to her husband."

"Exactly the scenario I had in mind."

Cecily forced a light laugh. "We sound like characters in one of those stories in the dreadful magazines my house-maids hide under their beds."

She had to admit to feeling a trifle breathless at the gleam in the doctor's expressive eyes.

"I was merely answering your question," he said innocently, while his wicked smile made her pulse beat faster.

"Indeed you were." She dropped her gaze, wondering why it was that the man always managed to make her feel confused. "And I thank you for sharing your opinion with me. But now I must be off. I have an engagement at Dolly's."

He looked momentarily disappointed, then he flashed her a smile and doffed his hat. "Good day, Cecily. I enjoyed our encounter immensely. I hope we can repeat it soon."

She nodded at him and, after a brief wave of her hand, ordered Samuel to commence with the journey.

Dr. Prestwick had taken up residency in Badgers End only recently, but already he had half the women in the village swooning over him.

While she did not include herself in their company, Cecily had to confess to a certain fluttering of her heart whenever he spoke to her. That kind of charm was dangerous, she well knew. And it irritated her that she was susceptible to it. The man always made her feel guilty about the most innocent of encounters.

Though why she should feel guilty about any meeting with him, she had yet to discover. Why she should think of Baxter in the same context, she had not the faintest idea. Impatient with her fanciful notions that made no sense, she concentrated on the pleasure of her lunch with Phoebe.

The silver bell hanging on the door of Dolly's Tea Shop jangled loudly as Cecily entered a few minutes later. The room vibrated with the sounds of laughing voices and soft laughter, the tinkle of teacups against saucers and of teaspoons in silver sugar bowls.

Phoebe had already arrived and was ensconced in the usual corner by the fireplace, which today displayed a colorful bouquet of gladioli and lilies, instead of the leaping flames of the coal fire that usually warmed the tearoom in the winter.

Phoebe smiled and waved as Cecily eased her way between the tables, past chattering ladies and bored-looking gentlemen. The enticing aroma of freshly baked bread produced a faint growl in her stomach, and she looked forward with pleasurable anticipation to enjoying some of Dolly's currant buns with her tea.

"Do sit down," Phoebe said impatiently when Cecily reached the table. "I've ordered a tray of pastries and tea. It should be here any minute. Dolly tells me she has some fresh Devonshire cream, so I ordered scones as well."

Feeling quite ravenous at this news, Cecily took her seat at the table and began to remove her gloves. "Tell me, did you manage to rehearse this morning?" she asked as she eased the long tight fabric over her fingers.

"Yes, we did. Fortunately there was no sign of the constable, so we were undisturbed. Which was just as well. My dear, these girls are absolutely hopeless. Dora yawned through the entire ordeal. She complained that she hadn't had a wink of sleep the night before because an owl kept hooting in the woods behind her house."

"Owls can be quite bothersome at times," Cecily murmured. She peeled off the second glove and laid them both in her lap.

"These young girls should be able to sleep through anything. I know I could when I was their age. It wasn't until after dear Sedgely died that I had trouble sleeping. I would wake up night after night in that empty bed, feeling a sense of loss. When one has slept with a person for a number of years, it is difficult to adjust to sleeping alone again."

Cecily silently agreed with her. It had taken weeks before she had become accustomed to sleeping alone after James had died. It would seem that, even though her mind was not conscious, the sense of loneliness could be so acute as to penetrate and arouse her from the deepest slumber.

"Anyway," Phoebe went on, "I eventually managed to get some sense of order drummed into those hapless women. You wouldn't believe the interruptions. It seemed as though every two minutes or so someone would have an excuse to disrupt the rehearsal. Marion needed to venture into the privacy of the woods to relieve herself and of course was afraid to go alone, so two of them had to go with her. No sooner was she back than someone else had to go, and back and forth they trooped until I told them that if anyone else had to go, they would simply have to do it out there in the open. That shut them up for a while, but then . . ."

Phoebe prattled on while Cecily listened with only half an ear. She was thinking about Lord Sherbourne and how he had slept so soundly he hadn't missed his wife until the following morning.

CHAPTER

❈ 14 ❈

"Anyway," Phoebe said, "one good thing came out of all their shenanigans, apart from the fact that we did achieve somewhat moderate success in the dancing." She reached for the small silk purse attached to her belt and loosened the drawstring. "Now where did I put the dratted thing?"

Dolly chose that moment to arrive, carrying a tray laden with appetizing pastries. Her fleshy double chins wobbled as she said breathlessly, "Be back in a minute with the tea." She dumped the tray on the table and straightened, one fleshy hand reaching for her back. "I'm getting too old for this lark," she muttered.

Cecily looked at her in sympathy. She knew all about aching backs. "Where is Katie today? Is she not well?"

"Gone to the Smoke to live, hasn't she." Dolly shook her head, waggling her chins again. "It's where they all go, soon as they turn fourteen. Off to London to see the bloody king.

Never mind leaving me to carry on by meself with the Season coming up and all."

"Well, they earn so much money in service nowadays," Phoebe said, helping herself to a creamy eclair. "Especially with some of the better families. Quite a pampered life compared to some, I'd say."

"It ain't the money they go for," Dolly said with a loud sniff. "They go up there hoping to get their skinny little hands on a toff, that's what. Find a rich husband. That's all these girls think about anymore. Forget the hardships of working on the farm with your old man. No wonder so many farms are going under. There's no one to run them."

"Well," Phoebe said, the plumes on her hat waving up and down, "there is something to be said for a better life. It's as they say, Dolly, it's just as easy to love a rich man as a poor one."

"And there's those who are too young to know the difference between love and lust," Dolly said, slapping her hands together as if brushing off the entire younger generation. "Lord knows where I'll find another girl to work for me."

She looked down at the tray with a start. "Well, I can't stand here nattering. I'll be back with your tea in a jiff." She turned her massive back on them and jostled her way through the tables to the kitchen.

"Poor Dolly," Cecily said, looking after her. "It must be so difficult for her. I know how hard it is to find help."

"Well, I think you are most fortunate to have such good people working for you," Phoebe said. "It isn't often one comes across such loyalty to one's employer."

"If you treat them well, you'll get the best from them," Cecily said, eyeing the currant buns. She couldn't decide between one of those and the slice of Dundee cake with the glacé cherries and whole almonds.

"Well, I'm not so sure about that. I mean, no one treats those silly dancers better than I do. And what thanks do I get? They make silly jokes and giggle to the point where they have to keep running into the forest to wee."

Phoebe's expression changed to one of dismay, and she

covered her mouth with her fingers. "Horrors! The little monsters have me speaking like them now. I do beg your pardon, Cecily. I can't imagine what I was thinking of."

Amused by this uncharacteristic slip, Cecily said lightly, "Do not concern yourself, Phoebe. I'm sure it won't happen again."

"I certainly hope not. Can you imagine Algie's face if he heard his mother use such language? Why, it's enough to make dear Sedgely turn in his grave. Oh, which reminds me."

She dug her fingers into the tiny silk purse and withdrew a small round box. "One of the girls found this pillbox at the edge of the woods while they were . . . er . . . occupied. As you can see, there is an initial *B* carved into the lid. Since it is of good quality gold, and considering where it was found, I assume it must have belonged to Lady Sherbourne. I don't know if the police should have it, or perhaps you should give it to Lord Sherbourne."

Cecily took the tiny gold box and examined it. The initial had been ornately carved, with a flourish of palm leaves and tiny scrolls. "I will give it to Lord Sherbourne for safekeeping," she said, "but I will also mention it to the inspector whenever he can find the time to question my guests."

"He hasn't done so as yet?" Phoebe asked in surprise.

Cecily shook her head. "I'm very much afraid our time is running out, unless we can persuade him to release his quarantine on the Downs by tomorrow. Perhaps, once he has questioned the gypsies and found nothing of any interest, he will consider allowing us to proceed with our plans for the festivities."

"You don't believe the murderer came from the gypsy camp?" Phoebe's eyes widened, and she leaned forward, one feather curling in front of her face. "Who do you think it was, then?" she whispered.

"I have not the faintest idea," Cecily whispered back.

"Oh." Phoebe looked intensely disappointed. "Well, whoever it is, I certainly hope they apprehend the man in very short order. You simply can't imagine what a dreadful feeling that was, to be dancing gaily around a maypole

which just two short days ago was adorned with a dead
body. Gruesome, my dear. Absolutely gruesome. I quite
expected to see a swarthy villain with a knife in his teeth
come dashing out of the woods at any moment."

She sniffed and hunted in her sleeve for her handkerchief.

Cecily took the opportunity to lift the small box to her
nose before tucking it inside the pocket of her skirt. She
wasn't really surprised by the aroma she had detected.

Ever since she had first recognized the initial on the lid as
the Boscombe family crest, she had suspected that the
container was not a pillbox, as Phoebe had surmised. It was,
as her nose had confirmed, a gentleman's snuffbox. It
undoubtedly belonged to a member of the Boscombe
family.

Phoebe reached for a scone and delicately slit it in half
with a pearl-handled knife. She then lavishly spread one half
with the Devonshire cream and the other half with straw-
berry jam. After fitting the two pieces together again, she
sliced off a piece and popped it into her mouth.

"Wonderful," she declared, a look of rapture creeping
over her face.

Watching her, Cecily felt an irresistible urge to taste a
scone. Sighing, she reached for one, vowing to resist
Phoebe's next invitation to the tea shop. How the woman
kept her wasp waist squeezed into that impossible corset
when she consumed pastries the way a furnace consumed
coal was beyond her understanding.

Looking up, Cecily saw Dolly charging toward them,
cups rattling on the tray in her hands. She seemed not to
notice as her hips brushed elbows and tables on her clumsy
course across the room.

"Sorry it took so long." She gasped, dumping the tray
with a clatter on the table. One beefy hand swiped at her
sweaty brow. "Do you have enough scones there?"

"Plenty," Cecily said firmly. "And the cream is delicious,
as I knew it would be. One of my guests enjoyed it for tea
two days ago and commented on the quality of the Devonshire cream."

"Two days ago?" Dolly frowned. "Who was that, then?"

"Arthur Boscombe. He mentioned that he called in here after a long walk along the Esplanade. It would have been midafternoon, I shouldn't wonder."

Dolly gave an emphatic shake of her head. "No, no, Mrs. Sinclair. You must have been misinformed. There were only locals in here two days ago. I know, because that was the day Katie left, and I was that thankful I didn't have a big crowd in. I would certainly have known if one of the Boscombe family had been in here. Can't hardly miss them, can you?"

Cecily smiled. "Indeed, you can't, Dolly. Perhaps I had the day wrong."

"Must have done, I reckon." Dolly looked up as the bell jangled. "Can you believe they are still coming in? I don't know how I'm going to take care of this lot on my own, I swear I don't." Grumbling and muttering, she took off for the kitchen.

Interesting, Cecily thought, fingering the snuffbox inside her pocket. That made yet another member of the Boscombe family who had something to hide. She was beginning to wonder if any of them had told her the truth. Now she had a few more questions to ask, and the answers should be most interesting.

Gertie sat on the settee, poring over the knitting pattern that Mrs. Chubb had given her. It had belonged to her daughter and had so many creases in it Gertie could hardly read it. "Purl two, knit two," she muttered to herself, "b-w-f . . . what the bleeding hell is b-w-f?"

Glaring at the knitting needles she held in one hand as if it were their fault, she said crossly, "Bloody well futile, that's what that means. How am I supposed to follow this pattern if I can't read the flipping directions? Now I'll have to go and ask Mrs. Chubb, and I'm going to look like a right idiot, aren't I."

The kitchen door slammed, and Gertie looked up, embarrassed at being caught talking to herself. The next minute she frowned as Ian appeared in the doorway.

"What're you doing home at this hour?" she demanded. "You ain't got the bleeding sack, have yer?"

Ian just stood there, looking at her, not saying a word.

Slowly she put the pattern and needles down on the settee next to her and stood up. "What's the matter?" Her voice had become louder, but she was too worried to control it. "What's wrong with you? You look as if you swallowed a winkle and found out it was a slug."

Ian opened his mouth, shut it again, lifted his hands, and let them drop.

Thoroughly alarmed now, Gertie stared at her husband's pinched white face. "Here," she said, starting forward. "There ain't been another murder, has there? Who's been murdered now, then?"

Ian shook his head. "Gertie," he said, then stopped as a shuffling sound came from behind him.

Gertie stared in amazement at the woman who stood just behind his shoulder. She recognized her at once. The woman she'd seen hanging around the foyer the day before. "Hello," Gertie said, not knowing what else to say.

"Hello." The woman looked at her with such a sorrowful expression in her big brown eyes that Gertie couldn't help feeling sorry for her. She looked like she hadn't eaten in months, her cheeks all sunken in like that. Make three of her, she would, Gertie thought, trying to ignore the creepy feeling that bothered her stomach.

"Who is she, then?" Gertie asked Ian without taking her eyes off the bony face.

"She's . . . Her name is Gloria," Ian said.

"Gloria Johnson," the woman echoed right behind him.

The sinking feeling in Gertie's stomach was getting worse. "All right," she said, her voice sharpening. "But who is she, Ian? What does she want?"

Ian's mouth flapped open like a fish out of water. "She's . . . she's . . ."

"His wife," the strange girl obligingly finished for him.

Gertie heard the words, but they were so ridiculous she ignored them. "What do you want?" she demanded, deciding that the direct attack was the best approach.

"Gertie," Ian said in a voice she'd never heard him use before, "she's right. She's my wife."

Gertie jammed her fists into her hips. "Don't be bleeding daft, Ian Rossiter. How can she be your wife? I'm your bloody wife, remember?"

"His name isn't Ian Rossiter," the girl said. "It's Robert Johnson."

Gertie looked desperately at Ian's face. The face she'd known and loved for two years. The face she'd married. The face she'd blinking done it with every night for the last three months. Why wasn't he calling this crazy woman a liar? Why was he standing there looking at her as if she'd turned into a baboon with two faces?

Because she was having a bloody nightmare. Wasn't she? It wasn't real. Was it? "Ian?" she said faintly.

He took a step forward, stopped, and said quietly, "I'm sorry, Gertie. I hoped you'd never find out."

"No," Gertie whispered. "No, I don't bloody believe it." Yet, looking into his eyes, she knew she did.

"I've been looking for him for two months," the strange woman called Gloria said. "He used to come home every weekend, then all of a sudden he stopped coming. I didn't know if he was alive or dead. But I had to find out, didn't I?"

Every weekend. Ian had gone up to London every weekend since she'd known him. Until two months ago when she'd insisted he stay home with her. "Bloody hell," she whispered. "And I'm bleeding pregnant."

"So am I," Gloria said, looking as if she wanted to cry. "That's why I had to find him."

Gertie ignored her. "Why?" she said as her stomach started clenching like a fist. "Why the hell did you do it?"

Ian shrugged. "I got in a spot of bother in the Smoke and had to get out in a hurry. I told Gloria I'd lie low for a bit, but I promised I'd come home every weekend. Well, I did. For two years. But then I met you and, well, I wanted to marry you. I didn't love her anymore."

Behind him, Gloria started weeping in a helpless way that tore at Gertie's heart. "You loved her enough to get her bleeding pregnant, Ian—whatever your name is. The same bleeding time you was getting me that way, too. How could you do that to me? And to her? How bleeding well could you, you bastard?"

She felt like crying herself. But not yet. Not in front of the man she'd thought was her husband, and the poor fish who was his wife. She was too bleeding angry to cry. What she wanted to do was kill him. But that wasn't getting her anywhere.

Ian held up a shaking hand. "Gertie, wait—"

"Don't you bleeding wait me." She squared her shoulders, ready to belt him one if he made one move toward her. "Get out of here, you lying bastard. You find the guts to face the music and go home with your bloody wife, where you bleeding belong. I don't know what I'm going to do yet, but I tell you one thing. You ain't never going to set eyes on this child. Never. Nor me neither. Now get out, and bleeding good riddance."

He stared at her for a long moment, while she stared back, willing herself not to buckle in. Then, with a loud sigh, he turned his back and left, with Gloria trailing behind him.

Gertie waited until she heard the door shut quietly behind them. Then she sat down onto the settee and bawled.

Cecily returned to the hotel that afternoon, anxious to have another word with Arthur Boscombe. After the brisk walk along the Esplanade, she felt revived and clear-headed, and ready to tackle just about anything. The snuffbox would have to be handed over to the police, of course, but there was no reason at all why she shouldn't first determine who the owner was.

She was disappointed when she saw Arthur had joined in a croquet game, together with his wife. She had been hoping for an opportunity to talk to him alone. She could still ask him about the snuffbox, however, and his answer should tell her what she wanted to know.

The game was a long one, and Cecily had grown quite weary of it by the time it was over. Arthur seemed to have lost his former melancholy and even joked with his wife, obviously pleased with his victory.

As they started to walk back to the hotel, Cecily caught up with them, saying pleasantly, "You played a wonderful game, Lord Arthur. I quite enjoyed watching you trounce your opponents in such a forthright manner."

"Thank you, Mrs. Sinclair, I'm sure." His smile seemed quite genuine, and even Grace looked elated.

"I was wondering if you could spare me a minute," Cecily said with an apologetic smile at Lady Grace. "There is something I wish to show you."

"Certainly, madam, I shall be happy to," Arthur said, though he looked a little apprehensive.

He paused, his wife's hand on his arm, and waited while Cecily withdrew the small round box from her pocket. "I do believe this is the family crest, is it not?" she asked, holding the box so that he could see the lid.

"It is indeed," Arthur said, looking taken aback. "Might I ask where you found it?"

"I picked it up in the Rose Garden," Cecily said, hoping she wouldn't be punished for telling the small lie. "I thought I recognized the Boscombe family emblem, and I wondered if perhaps the snuffbox might belong to you."

Arthur shook his head. "Never use the stuff, madam. Filthy habit, if you ask me. Does dreadful things to one's nose, you know. My father gave all three of his sons an identical box. Mine is safely tucked away in the sideboard at home."

"Yes, that's right, it is," Grace confirmed with a nod of her head.

"I see. Then the box must belong to one of your brothers." Cecily turned the snuffbox over in her hand. "Do either of them use snuff?"

"Well, I know they did at one time," Arthur said, stroking his chin. "Of course, I don't know if they do as of now. I haven't noticed either of them using the stuff lately. It really is quite a messy habit."

"Oh, I have seen them, Arthur dear," Grace said, giving Cecily a bright smile. "I saw Sylvester use some the other night after dinner. I know Deirdre wasn't at all happy with him. He sat there and must have sneezed for a good fifteen minutes, one after the other. Poor Deirdre was most embarrassed."

"Can you remember which night that was?" Cecily asked, noting Arthur's sudden tension.

Grace thought about it. "It must have been at least four days ago. Poor dear Barbara was sitting with us, I know. It was the last night we were all together. I remember she commented on Sylvester's face when he was sneezing. She laughed at him, and Deirdre didn't like that at all."

"What about Lord Sherbourne," Cecily said. "Does he use snuff, too?"

"Well, I haven't seen him too often. The men usually wait until the ladies have left the table before indulging in all their unfavorable habits. That is why Deirdre was so upset with Sylvester. I do believe he'd imbibed too much wine that night."

"I see," Cecily said. "Well, then, perhaps I'll simply ask Sylvester if this is his box."

"Oh, well, I do know that Radley still uses snuff on occasion," Grace went on, as if she hadn't heard the words Cecily had spoken. "I happened to hear him ask Deirdre to buy him some two days ago when she went to the shops."

"Well, in that case, I'll ask them both if it's their box," Cecily said with a smile. "I'm sure whichever one of your brothers dropped it must have missed it by now. It looks quite valuable."

"It is indeed," Arthur said, squinting his eyes to get a better look at it. "I am sure either Sylvester or Radley would be most upset at the thought of its loss. Whoever owns it, I know he will be extremely happy that you found it. Most happy indeed."

Cecily thanked him and bade them both a good afternoon. For once she had to disagree with Arthur Boscombe. Whichever one of the brothers had dropped the snuffbox, he was not likely to be at all happy that it had been found. Particularly when he learned exactly where it had been located.

CHAPTER

❊15❊

As usual, Sylvester Boscombe proved to be as elusive as ever. Spying Lady Deirdre alone in the drawing room, Cecily approached her and politely inquired as to the whereabouts of her husband.

"I am afraid I can't help you," Deirdre said in a bored voice. "I imagine he is either taking his daily stroll along the sands, or he is with his brother in Radley's suite. I'm afraid Radley is taking the death of his wife extremely hard. My husband has spent a great deal of time lately attempting to comfort him."

"I can imagine how the poor man must be suffering," Cecily said quietly. "Perhaps when you see your husband, you will tell him there is a small matter I wish to discuss with him."

Deirdre eyed her curiously, though she did her best to hide her interest when she said, "I will pass on your message as soon as I meet with Sylvester again, which will most likely be at dinner this evening.''

"Thank you. I would greatly appreciate that.''

"Do you have any idea how long it will be before we are allowed to return to the city?'' Deirdre tossed her head, and the sunlight caught the diamond clasp in her hair, sending a blinding flash of light across Cecily's face. "I had planned on returning on Saturday, but now I understand we have to wait until we have been questioned by the police.''

"I apologize for the inconvenience, milady. As a matter of fact, I had hoped the inspector would have called here by now. Unfortunately he was delayed in London for a day or two and is at present conducting his investigation at the gypsy encampment. I'm quite sure that once he has completed his inquiries there, he will make haste to proceed with his questioning of the members of your family.''

"Yes, well, I do hope he finds what he is looking for at the gypsy camp, and then we can all be spared the ordeal of rehashing this dreadful tragedy.''

"While I share your sentiments, Lady Deirdre, I doubt very much if the inspector will solve this case by investigating the gypsies.''

Deirdre gave her a sharp look. "And pray what do you mean by that?''

Cecily moved over to the door and closed it, giving them a little more privacy. "I am convinced,'' she said, returning to seat herself in an armchair, "that Lady Sherbourne was not killed by a gypsy.''

Deirdre looked startled. "How can you be certain of that, may I ask?''

"There were no bruises on the body. No sign of a struggle. That would suggest that your sister-in-law was familiar with the person who attacked her. She must have been taken by surprise and had no chance to put up any resistance. Once the killer had her trussed helplessly by the ribbons, it would have been a simple matter to wind one more around her neck, thereby strangling her.''

Deirdre shuddered visibly. "That really doesn't surprise me a great deal. Barbara would have let any man close to her, had he been the least bit attractive to her. She wasn't too discriminating as far as admirers were concerned. It mattered not to her whether they were married or betrothed. It was a sport to her, and she reveled in it."

Taking advantage of this sudden willingness to share confidences, Cecily said quietly, "You were, perhaps, referring to your own husband?"

The other woman's face flamed, and she looked away to where the huge bay window overlooked the ocean. "I am not defending my husband," she said, a trace of bitterness underlying her words. "Like most attractive men, he is vulnerable in certain areas. He has a great deal of difficulty ignoring the advances of a beautiful woman. While I admit he is susceptible to flattery and attention, that was not so in the case of my sister-in-law."

"So Lady Sherbourne did pay attention to your husband?"

Deirdre made an angry gesture with her hand. "She threw herself at him. Sylvester can't be blamed for that, he is an attractive man. As I have said, he had his weaknesses, as do all men, but he certainly drew the line at any involvement with his brother's wife."

"So he rejected her amorous overtures?"

"He would have nothing whatsoever to do with her."

"I imagine that Lady Sherbourne would have been put out about that."

Deirdre uttered a tight laugh. "Put out? Those are small words for what that woman did to my husband. She did her level best to bring about disgrace on him and the family. She threatened to go to Lord Sherbourne with the story that Sylvester had forced himself on her one night, and that he had had his way with her."

Cecily knew her expression registered shock. "Oh, my. That must have been a dreadful worry for him."

"And for me. I was furious when he told me. I was filled with loathing for the woman. I wanted to tell Radley exactly what kind of woman he was married to, but Sylvester dissuaded me. He said that Radley was so in love with his wife, he would never believe a word against her, and that he would blame Sylvester for everything that had happened. So I was forced to keep quiet about it."

Cecily watched the woman's face carefully. It was obvious that Deirdre had hated her sister-in-law, but Cecily didn't think this elegant, sophisticated woman was capable of murder. "Did Lady Sherbourne ever carry out her threat to incriminate your husband?" she asked.

"No. We would certainly have known if she had. Radley would have taken a sword to him, no doubt. Sylvester told me he had managed to persuade Barbara to let the matter rest."

"Your husband must have a most persuasive manner," Cecily said, wondering what it was Sylvester had said to defuse the situation.

Deirdre sighed, her gaze still on the view outside. "I must confess I was surprised that he had succeeded in keeping her quiet. Once Barbara set her mind on something, a herd of elephants couldn't shake her."

"Under the circumstances, I am surprised that Lady Sherbourne expressed interest in visiting the shops with you that afternoon."

Deirdre turned her face sharply to look at Cecily. "I've already told you, she made no such wish known to me. Had she done so, I would not have accepted her company. We did our best to avoid any physical contact with each other."

"Lord Sherbourne was under the impression that you and his wife were the best of friends."

"Radley could be very obtuse when it came to his wife." Deirdre returned her gaze to the window once more. "And I'm quite sure Barbara would have kept up the pretense, to avoid having to answer to her husband as to the nature of our disagreement."

The room was quiet for a moment while Cecily mulled over what she had heard. Outside, the *clip-clop* of horses mingled with the creak of the traps they pulled, while the frantic cries of the seagulls suggested some caring person had decided to feed them.

"You said that your husband told you that Lady Sherbourne intended to play croquet that afternoon?" Cecily inquired as the hoofbeats faded.

"Yes. I questioned him about that afterward. He said that she had intended to play, but the game was postponed because the gardener was cutting the grass."

"Ah, yes," Cecily said, nodding. "Now I remember. John mentioned cutting the grass that afternoon."

She tucked her fingers into her pocket and withdrew the round gold object. "Lady Deirdre," she said, handing the snuff box to her, "I believe your husband owns a box like this. Have you by any chance seen him use it lately?"

Deirdre looked at the box in her hand. "It's Sylvester's snuffbox. At least, it's either his or Radley's. They have identical boxes. Where did you find it?" She turned the box over, but at that moment the door opened abruptly.

Cecily felt a jolt of apprehension when she saw Lord Sherbourne standing in the doorway, his face contorted with anger.

"Mrs. Sinclair," he said, his voice vibrating like rolls of thunder, "I must emphatically protest this flagrant abuse of my wishes. I specifically warned you against harassing members of my family."

He entered the room as Cecily rose to her feet, his eyes flashing fire.

"Radley," Deirdre began, but he silenced her with a quick thrust of his hand.

"Might I remind you, madam, that the recent death of my wife is a traumatic and unbearable tragedy. We are all suffering intense grief and torment, and to be exposed to such insensitivity is unconscionable."

"My apologies, Lord Sherbourne," Cecily said evenly. "I was merely asking Lady Deirdre if the snuffbox I had found belonged to her husband. I had no wish to subject anyone to unnecessary pain."

"Then kindly do us the favor of leaving us alone to mourn the death of my beloved wife. I am afraid if you do not concur with my wishes, I shall be forced to complain of your conduct to the inspector, if and when he has the decency to get this intolerable investigation over with."

"I will do my best to see that the matter is taken care of at the earliest moment possible," Cecily said, crossing the room to the door. "In the meantime, please rest assured that the hotel and its staff are at your disposal for anything you might need."

She looked back before closing the door, but neither Lord Sherbourne nor his sister-in-law appeared to notice. Their attention seemed to be riveted on the snuffbox held in Lady Deirdre's hand.

Mrs. Chubb looked up as the kitchen door burst open, then slammed with an almighty crash against the wall. Her hand flew up to cover her mouth when she caught sight of Gertie standing there. Her hair flew all over the place, her shawl had been dragged off one shoulder, and she had the wildest look in her eyes Mrs. Chubb had ever seen.

"Good heavens, child, whatever has happened to you?" The housekeeper hurried forward and took her arm, her alarm growing when she felt the shudder vibrating from Gertie's body.

It was obvious from the housemaid's red-rimmed eyes that she had been crying. "Sit down here, duck. I'll fetch the brandy bottle." She settled the shivering Gertie into a chair and rushed over to the cupboard where Michel kept the best brandy. After uncorking the bottle, she poured some into a cup and brought it back to where Gertie sat, looking as if she could see the end of the world.

"Here," Mrs. Chubb said, thrusting the cup into her lifeless hand. "Drink that up."

She finally had to guide the cup to Gertie's trembling lips and force her to drink. It did the trick. Gertie coughed and spluttered, and then with a shudder pushed the cup away. "Strewth," she muttered, "that bleeding burns."

Mrs. Chubb studied her ravaged face. "I don't know what you've been crying about," she said, putting the cup down on the table. "But whatever it is, it can't be that bad." A sudden thought struck her, and she leaned forward, her hand on Gertie's arm. "Here, you haven't been attacked by one of them gypsies, have you?"

Gertie shook her head violently, tried to speak, and burst into tears instead.

"Gertie, for heaven's sake . . ." Mrs. Chubb broke off as another thought surfaced. "The baby? Oh, dear God, nothing has happened to the baby, has it?"

"No-o-o," Gertie sobbed. "I wish it bleeding had."

"Gertie, my girl, you bite your tongue!" Shocked beyond belief, Mrs. Chubb reached for the cup again. "Here, have another shot of this and tell me what happened."

Gertie shook her head and pressed her lips together.

"You're not going to tell me?"

"I will in a minute," Gertie said on a loud wail. "Just don't keep on at me."

Mrs. Chubb sighed and sat down on the other side of the table. In all the years she had known the child, since Gertie was twelve years old, she had never seen her in such a state. It had to be something terrible. But what it could be she couldn't imagine.

She waited patiently while Gertie gulped and sobbed, and then gradually quieted down. Then she said gently, "Do you feel like telling me now?"

Gertie nodded. "It's Ian," she said, her voice trembling on the name.

"He's ill? Someone said he'd gone home early. Have you called Dr. Prestwick? He'll know—"

Again she broke off as Gertie gave an impatient shake of her head. "He's not ill."

Mrs. Chubb frowned. "Then what is he?"

She jumped when Gertie opened her mouth and let out another wail. "He's bleeding married, that's what."

The housekeeper waited impatiently through the fresh bout of weeping. This was getting quite ridiculous. "I know he's married, dear," she said when the sobs subsided once more. "I was at the wedding, wasn't I. I saw you and him get married right there in the church."

"He ain't bloody married to me," Gertie said between hiccups. "Not legal, anyhow."

Mrs. Chubb reached for the cup and took a sip of brandy.

None of this was making sense. At least, she hoped it wasn't. "What do you mean, dear, it's not legal?"

"What I bleeding said. It ain't legal. For one thing, his name ain't bleeding Ian Rossiter. It's Johnson."

Where had she heard that name before? Mrs. Chubb wondered. She thought hard for a moment, then it came to her. The helpless-looking waif in the threadbare clothes and velvet hat. *I'm looking for Robert Johnson,* she'd said. "Oh, my god," Mrs. Chubb whispered.

"Too bleeding right," Gertie said bitterly. "He was already married, wasn't he. To some bleeding tart in London. Changed his name and came down here because he was in trouble with the law. Then what's he do? Meets up with me, don't he. Decides he wants to get married again and forgets to tell me he's already got a bleeding wife."

"No wonder he was upset about the baby." Mrs. Chubb shook her head. "I would never have believed it of him. Never in a hundred years. Where is he now?"

"On his way back to bleeding London, I hope. I told him I don't never want to see him again, and if he thinks he's getting his hands on my baby . . . I told him he's got another bloody think coming."

She looked up, and the look in her dark eyes near on broke Mrs. Chubb's heart. "What am I going to do?" she whispered. "How am I going to look after a baby and myself without no one to take care of us? What's going to happen to us?"

Mrs. Chubb rocked back and forth while she thought. "What about your father? Won't he help you?"

Gertie's laugh sounded bitter. "How's he going to help me? He ain't got nothing. He can hardly keep himself. And if I went to him I'd have to go back to the city. That ain't no place for a baby. And besides, me dad has a temper. He used to hit me when I was a kid. I ain't going to let him do that to my baby. I'd kill him if he touched it."

"There should be a law against men like Ian Rossiter," Mrs. Chubb muttered. "Too easy it is for them. He should be made to pay for that baby's upbringing."

"Yeah, well, that ain't going to help me any. Besides, his

wife's having a baby, too." Gertie buried her face in her hands. "Cor blimey, what a mess. I hate men. I'll never look at another blinking man again as long as I bloody live. I hate all the bastards."

"*Mon Dieu*, such language," a sharp voice said from the doorway.

Mrs. Chubb sent a warning look at Michel as he stalked into the kitchen, his tall white hat bobbing at every step. "She's upset, Michel, and for good reason. Leave her alone."

To her surprise, the chef paused by the table and patted Gertie awkwardly on the shoulder. "I heard. And I am sorry, Gertie. But that man, he is a rotter, and he is not worth the tears."

"I loved him so much," Gertie said, tears running down her cheeks.

"But you do not love him anymore, yes?" Michel waved an expressive hand in the air. "So you get back on your feet, look the world in the eye, and you say to hell with him. I get on with my life and I do better without him. No?"

"I could do a lot bleeding better without him if I didn't have a bun in the oven."

Michel threw both hands up in the air. "Oh, mercy me. Don't even think the words. The baby is the most precious thing a woman will ever have. We will find a way, Michel and Mrs. Chubb together. You are not to worry. Perhaps you can have your old room back at the hotel, yes?"

He looked meaningfully at Mrs. Chubb, who had sat staring at him with her mouth open. There was just no telling with Michel anymore. Full of surprises, he was. "I'll have a word with madam," she said. "I'm sure we can work out something."

Gertie's sobs eased up and she dragged her sleeve across her nose. "You think she'll let me come back? I can't afford to live in the cottage no more."

Mrs. Chubb nodded. "I shouldn't wonder at it. Don't worry, ducks. Like Michel says, we'll find a way."

Gertie looked up at the chef and smiled. "Thanks, Michel."

It wasn't much of a smile, but it brought color to the chef's cheeks. "Forget it," he said airily. "It is nothing. Now I get to work, yes? Or the dinner will not be on the tables for the savages." He looked up at the clock. "It is your day off today, no?"

Gertie nodded. "I'd better be getting back home."

"No, you stay." He lifted up a hand. "I cook you a special dinner. For you and the little one. You stay here and eat it, yes?"

A stray tear wandered down Gertie's cheek as she stared at him. "Michel," she said softly, "you are a bleeding angel."

He shrugged, but Mrs. Chubb could tell he was pleased as punch.

"You will not think so tomorrow when you are back here to work and I yell at you." His eye fell on the bottle standing on the table. "And what is this? You drink my best cognac? How I make the brandy truffles if the help sit there guzzling down the brandy?"

"She needed a little medicinal help," Mrs. Chubb said. "And so did I. Besides, we all know that more of that stuff finds its way down your gullet than it does in your precious truffles."

He stared at her for a moment, his eyebrows raised, then he reached for the bottle. Tipping back his head, he poured some brandy into his mouth and swallowed. "There. Now we are equal. So no more argument, yes?"

"Strewth," Gertie muttered. "How do you drink that stuff down like that without burning your guts out?"

Michel winked and in a perfect Cockney accent said, "Practice, me old darling. Bleeding practice."

CHAPTER 16

"You know, Baxter, the more I question the Boscombes, the more complicated the puzzle becomes." Cecily leaned across the library table to pinch off a dead bloom from the African violets. "I can't wait to see what the inspector makes of all this, if he ever gets here. I think Lord Sherbourne is getting very frustrated at the wait."

"I think," Baxter said, using his pompous voice, "it is far more likely that Lord Sherbourne is becoming frustrated by your attempts to solve the puzzle yourself. I can hardly blame him for losing his temper with you earlier. After all, he did ask you to refrain from harassing his family."

Cecily looked up in surprise. "Why, Baxter, that was a remarkably lengthy speech for you. And with a note of reprimand, I do believe. Are you feeling a little testy this afternoon? A little liverish, perhaps?"

"I am feeling perfectly well, madam, thank you. Just a

trifle concerned about your somewhat reckless actions at times."

"Piffle, Baxter. You worry too much. All I was doing was asking Lady Deirdre if she recognized the snuffbox as Sylvester's. She was about to tell me when Lord Sherbourne made his unexpected appearance. I shouldn't wonder if he was listening at the door. His interruption was certainly opportune."

"He most likely heard you interrogating a member of his family and rushed to the rescue."

Cecily sighed. "Well, I am still no closer to discovering the owner of the snuffbox. I do believe we can rule out Arthur, though. Although I would dearly love to know exactly where he was that afternoon, and why he had to lie about it. I think I shall have to confront him with his lie."

"Madam," Baxter said, his voice sharp, "I really do think you have done all you can. Perhaps it would be best now, in view of Lord Sherbourne's wrath, to leave any more questioning to Cranshaw."

"Simmer down, Baxter." Cecily folded her hands together and gave him a sweet smile. "I do have a possible theory. Would you care to hear it?"

"No doubt you are going to inform me, in any case," Baxter said dryly.

"Indeed I am. In exchange for one of your cigars."

"I think you are smoking entirely too much. I cannot imagine what your son will think when he arrives home to see his mother puffing away like a steam train."

"He will most likely be horrified."

"As well he should be. I hope he has more success in curing you of this disgraceful habit than I have had."

"You smoke, Baxter, do you not?"

"I, madam, am a man."

"And that makes it less of a disgraceful habit for you? Why is that, pray?"

She could see by his face that he bitterly regretted treading in this forbidden territory.

He ran a finger around the inside of his collar and

stretched his neck. "As I have told you before, madam, I do not make the rules. I merely observe them."

"If a few more men had the courage to admit that these so-called rules are outdated, outlandish, and outrageous, then we women could be emancipated; and instead of having to hide behind walls and around corners, we would be left in peace to enjoy our lives as we see fit."

Baxter's eyebrows lifted in a gesture she knew well. "I shudder to think, madam, what the world would come to if women were to be treated as equal to men. Where would you be without the protection, guidance, and financial security offered by men?"

"Doing what I am doing, Baxter. Running my own business, being responsible for my own actions, without answering to anyone, save for the law."

"And sometimes you disregard even that, madam."

"Only when it is necessary to overcome these ridiculous morals forced upon me by society. In every respect, Baxter, I function as well as any man."

Baxter opened his mouth, then shut it again.

She was not about to let him off so lightly. "Come, come, Baxter," she said with a trace of irritation, "out with it. You surely have the courage of your convictions after such an impassioned speech on the superiority of men."

She watched with interest as a dull shade of red crept over his face. He cleared his throat twice, then said stiffly, "I was merely going to point out, madam, that you are an exception. Most women do not have your fortitude or your common sense."

Disarmed at once, she allowed her smile to break through. "Why, thank you, Baxter. I shall accept that as a compliment."

"It was meant as one, madam. I have often . . ."

For a moment his gaze tangled with hers. She was aware of the same breathless feeling she had felt on occasion before, when he had looked at her in that same way.

"Yes?" she said softly. "You have often . . . ?"

He raised a hand to his mouth and coughed. "It is no

matter, madam. I do believe you were about to share your theory on the subject of Lord Arthur's whereabouts?"

She frowned, momentarily at a loss as to what he referred, and more than a little disappointed that he did not complete his sentence.

"Oh, the theory," she said, pulling her mind with difficulty back to the subject at hand. "Actually it wasn't to do with Arthur Boscombe. I was thinking of Sylvester and his association with Lady Sherbourne. Let us suppose, for instance, that Lady Deirdre was lying, and that Sylvester had indeed dallied with his sister-in-law."

Baxter made a slight sound, but Cecily was too involved in her scenario to take much notice. "Suppose, then, that Sylvester had tired of the game and wanted to look for fresh challenges, being the young stud that he is. Suppose he attempted to break off the relationship. Isn't it possible that Lady Sherbourne would then have a legitimate threat to expose him to her husband? It would certainly give Sylvester a motive to silence her."

She looked up and met Baxter's confused gaze. His face was scarlet, and she stared at him in surprise. "Is something the matter?"

"I find it a trifle uncomfortable to discuss this subject with you, madam."

"I don't understand why. We have discussed matters like this before, have we not?"

"That was before—"

She waited, anxious to hear the rest of his sentence. When none appeared forthcoming, she gently prompted, "Before what, Baxter?"

To her intense disappointment, he said quickly, "I regret to end this discussion, madam, but I have a pressing engagement I have to attend to in just a few minutes. If you will forgive me?"

She sighed. "Very well. I do wish I could have solved this puzzle by now. I have to admit, I am becoming very discouraged. Yet, somewhere in the back of my mind, I have the feeling I already have the answer. I just can't put a finger on it."

Baxter looked apprehensive. "Will you promise me, madam, that you will not risk angering Lord Sherbourne any further? I should hate to see him complain to the inspector."

"I have no wish to see him do that either," Cecily said, rising to her feet. "But I have to pursue this until the very end of the trail. I am not one to give up, as you well know."

"I do indeed," Baxter said mournfully.

She smiled at him as she passed him. "Well, you can be thankful for one thing this time, Bax. So far I haven't involved you in any wild escapades."

"That is scant assurance," he muttered as he followed her out of the library. "Something tells me that you will do so, before this matter is over."

Halfway across the foyer, Cecily was surprised to see the front door open to admit Phoebe, who appeared to be in her usual agitated state. "Have you heard from the inspector yet?" she demanded as soon as she set eyes on Cecily. "Everyone is asking me if they will be allowed to set up tomorrow, and I have no answer for them."

She had no answer either, Cecily thought, but she wasn't about to let that deter her. "Tell them to proceed with whatever plans they had for tomorrow," she told Phoebe. "I will send word to the inspector that we intend to do so. He must have finished his investigation by now, and it can no longer be of any use to him to hold the Downs out-of-bounds."

"But what about the barriers?" Phoebe said, fanning herself with her handkerchief. "We had to remove them ourselves this morning. If people see them there, they may not care to ignore them."

"I will send Ian and Samuel along to remove them," Cecily said firmly. "Don't worry, Phoebe, I will take full responsibility. Please just inform everyone to proceed as planned. Badgers End shall have its May Day festivities as we have always done."

Phoebe clapped her hands in delight. "Wonderful. Thank you, Cecily. Now all that is left is to hope that those silly dancers remember the steps and refrain from going inside when they should be going outside. It's asking for a miracle, I admit, but the maypole shall have its ribbons threaded one way or another."

"Did I hear you say maypole, old bean?" a familiar voice trumpeted from the hallway.

Phoebe groaned. "I really must run," she whispered urgently. "Please make my apologies to the colonel." Before Cecily could answer, Phoebe scuttled across the foyer and out the door.

"By Jove, that woman can move fast," Colonel Fortescue said as he marched unsteadily forward. "Nice pair of ankles, considering her age, what?"

"I can't say that I've noticed," Cecily said primly. "Now if you'll excuse me——"

"She did mention the maypole, didn't she? I did hear correctly?" He stuck a finger in his ear and waggled it. "Never know these days. Hear so much stuff going on in there, I never know if it's in the ear or in the mind. Dashed miserable, this getting old business. Can't move the old bones like I once did."

"Colonel," Cecily said with a great deal of patience, "if you are wondering if the May Day dance will be performed as planned, all I can tell you at this point is that we certainly have every intention of continuing with our plans for the festivities."

"Well, that's a relief." He took a large white handkerchief from his breast pocket and mopped his sweaty brow. "I did wonder, seeing as how someone hung that poor woman on the ribbons. Wouldn't want to watch that happen on May Day, you know. Be blasted depressing that, what?"

"I don't think you need worry, Colonel. We are not likely to see that happen again."

"I should hope not." He blinked hard and rocked forward on his feet. Breathing a cloud of gin fumes into Cecily's face, he whispered, "I thought I'd found it, you know."

Holding her breath for a moment, Cecily frowned at him. "Found it?" she echoed when she considered it safe to breathe again.

"Yes. The blasted head. Behind the courtyard. Thimble's

compost heap. I took a shortcut from the ballroom to the bar last night, and there it was, sitting smack in the middle of the compost heap.''

"The head," Cecily said, trying to look as if she understood.

"Yes, madam. You know, the one belonging to *him.*"

"Him?"

The colonel rolled his bloodshot eyes at the ceiling. "The one belonging to the headless horseman. Remember? The blighter who came out of the dark at me that night without his blasted head, cape flying and on a horse breathing fire, by George.''

"Oh," Cecily said warily, "that head."

"Yes, madam. That head indeed. As soon as I saw it I thought"—he shot a finger in the air in front of his face—"Aha! There it is! It hadn't rolled into the sea after all.''

"I'm sure that was a relief, Colonel, to know where it was."

Once more his eyes rolled to the ceiling. He clasped his hands behind his back and rocked back on his heels at such a steep angle that Cecily became alarmed he'd lose his balance.

"Well, old bean, it would have been a great relief," he said as he rocked back again, sending his body tilting toward her so that they almost touched noses, "except it wasn't the blasted head after all.''

"It wasn't?" Feeling faint from the gust of alcohol, Cecily moved back. Out of the corner of her eye, she saw Arthur Boscombe cross the foyer, heading for the front door. And for once he was alone.

"No, by Jove, it wasn't," the colonel boomed. "You would never guess what it was. It looked for all the world like a man's head, white and squishy after lying in the sun. I've seen faces like that on the bodies of the Gurkhas. Eyes gone, all bloated up from the ants—"

"Colonel," Cecily said hurriedly, "I really must run, do forgive me—"

She started across the foyer, with the colonel bellowing

behind her, "It was a ruddy great cabbage, old bean. That's what it was, a ruddy cabb—"

Mercifully the door closed behind her, shutting off the strident voice.

Poised at the head of the steps, Cecily saw Arthur Boscombe across the street alongside the railing. He had begun a leisurely stroll and was just a few yards away.

Picking up her skirts, Cecily sprinted across the road and caught up with him.

He seemed uncomfortable when he saw her, as if he were expecting the meeting to be unpleasant. "Mrs. Sinclair," he said, politely doffing his hat. "Is something the matter?"

"I hope not, Lord Arthur," Cecily said breathlessly. "But there is a little matter that I hope you can clear up for me."

He sent a swift glance past her shoulder toward the hotel. "I have only a moment, I'm afraid. I have an appointment in the town."

He certainly hadn't been in that much of a hurry when she'd first spotted him, Cecily thought. Either Radley had warned him about talking to her, or he was worried about someone else seeing him.

"Well, I'll walk along with you for a little way so that you won't be late," she said, beginning to stride out in the direction of the town. "This should not take too long, in any case."

There was little that Arthur could do except fall in step alongside her, which he did, albeit reluctantly, judging from the expression on his face.

"Lord Arthur," Cecily said after they had traveled a few steps, "I happened to be in Dolly's Tea Shop today."

She felt his sudden start, but pretended she hadn't noticed.

"Oh, indeed?" he mumbled. "Wonderful food there. Especially the scones and clotted cream."

"Yes, I have to agree." Cecily waited for a few more steps. "As a matter of fact, I mentioned to Dolly that you had been in there two days ago." She glanced at him out of the corner of her eye. "The afternoon Lady Sherbourne was murdered."

After a long pause Arthur said in a thin voice, "And what did she tell you?"

Cecily looked at him, but he stared straight ahead with a grim expression on his face, marching as if into battle.

"I think you know what she said," Cecily said gently.

Arthur coughed and reached for his handkerchief. After wiping his mouth, he returned the square of linen to his breast pocket. "I imagine she told you I wasn't there that afternoon."

"That is precisely what she told me."

"And you, naturally, are wondering why I told you such a bunch of poppycock."

Cecily smiled. "I have to admit, the thought crossed my mind that perhaps you were engaged in something you wished to keep secret."

"Yes, well, that is correct." Arthur cleared his throat. "Mrs. Sinclair, if I confess to you, will you give me your solemn pledge you will not disclose what I am about to tell you? Particularly to my wife."

Cecily thought about that for a moment. It was fairly safe to assume that whoever had dropped the snuffbox was the person who had killed Lady Sherbourne. It could have been dropped by Barbara herself, of course, but then why would she carry with her a snuffbox belonging to her husband, or her brother-in-law, unless she was perhaps meeting one of them to return it?

In any case, Arthur's snuffbox was presumably at his home, stored away in the sideboard. Which would rule out his involvement in this affair.

Making up her mind, Cecily said, "You have my oath that I will not repeat what you tell me."

He was silent for a minute, then said, "I'll be honest, Mrs. Sinclair. Normally I would suggest you mind your own business. But since I am aware that you are making inquiries about the murder, and that each member of my family is suspect, I will give you the answer you seek. It will not only prove my innocence, but that of another member of the family as well."

"And I should remind you, Mr. Boscombe, that if what

you tell me has any bearing on the murder, you must repeat it to the police when they question you."

He sighed. "Yes, I was very much afraid of that. Very well, I will tell you." He lifted his chin, as if bracing for an unpleasant task. "I was extremely foolish, Mrs. Sinclair. I formed an unfortunate attachment to my brother's wife, Barbara. I am not proud of my obsession, and I made every attempt to extinguish the fires that burned in me every time I set eyes on her, but it was impossible."

Not quite certain how best to respond, Cecily murmured, "I'm sorry. I'm sure it must have been a cause of distress for you."

"Not only for me, but for my wife, who was aware of my weakness." He sighed. "On the day in question I had a conversation with Lord Sherbourne, during which he casually mentioned that his wife planned to go shopping with Deirdre that afternoon."

A nanny paused ahead of them at the railings, holding two small children by the hand. The breeze whipped her skirt about her ankles and ruffled the children's hair. She smiled down at them as they excitedly pointed out the ship lying at anchor out in the bay, and Cecily smiled wistfully with her. The boys reminded her of her own two sons when they were small, so long ago now.

Her spirits lifted when she remembered that Michael would be home soon, and she brought her concentration back to bear on Arthur's story.

He waited until they had passed by the small group before continuing. "I never missed an opportunity to spend some time with Barbara. So it was that afternoon. I followed Deirdre at a discreet distance, expecting her to meet up with Barbara at some point. She never did, of course. I waited all afternoon and then returned to the hotel shortly ahead of Deirdre."

Cecily nodded. "I see."

"Since I found it hard to explain my loitering in town for such a length of time, I told my wife I had called in for afternoon tea at the tea shop."

"That certainly does explain things. Thank you, Lord

Arthur, for confiding in me. That does appear to exonerate you and Lady Deirdre from any suspicion."

Arthur stopped and looked down at her with an earnest expression on his face. "Mrs. Sinclair, I am compelled to say this. I cannot imagine, for one single instant, that any member of my family could be capable of murder. I feel certain that the villain must have come from the gypsy encampment. That is the only thing that makes sense."

Cecily returned his gaze, wishing she could agree with him. "For the sake of your family, Lord Arthur, I sincerely hope that you are right."

She watched him walk away, his head bowed, obviously deep in morbid thoughts. So neither Deirdre nor Arthur had been on the Downs that afternoon. Grace had been in the Rose Gardens. That left only Sylvester and Radley.

She wrestled with the problem as she slowly walked back to the hotel in the early evening sunshine. There was still that nagging feeling in the back of her mind that she already had the answer.

She remembered the colonel, his hand flapping in the air as he talked about the headless horseman. *The blighter who came out of the dark at me that night without his blasted head, cape flying, and on a horse breathing fire.*

The image stayed in her mind as she climbed the steps to the front door. Something else popped into her mind, something Grace had said earlier that day. Something that didn't make sense.

Lifting her head to the darkening sky, Cecily let out a long, slow breath. Now, finally, she thought she knew who it was who had murdered Lady Sherbourne.

CHAPTER
✠ 17 ✠

Crossing the foyer a few minutes later, Cecily heard her name called. Mrs. Chubb had just reached the top of the kitchen stairs and seemed breathless as she hurried toward her.

"I'm so glad I caught you, mum. I wonder if I could have a word with you?"

"Of course." Cecily led the way down the hallway to the library, wondering what new problem had arisen. "I hope there is nothing wrong? Michel did arrive to cook the evening meal, didn't he?"

"Oh, yes, mum. In fine fettle, he is. He's clashing and banging around down there, like he always does when he's in a good mood."

"And especially when he's not," Cecily said dryly. She reached the door of the library and pushed it open. "There's no one in here at present, thank goodness, so we are assured of some privacy."

The room seemed chilled after the warm sunshine outside. She rubbed her arms, wishing she'd brought her shawl down with her. "Now, what is the trouble?" she asked as Mrs. Chubb hovered just inside the door.

"It's Gertie, mum. She's pregnant."

"Why, that's wonderful!" Cecily clasped her hands to bring them to her face. "I am so happy for her. She must be absolutely thrilled. A baby! Just imagine, Gertie with a baby. It really doesn't seem that long ago that she was just a child herself."

"Yes, mum. Well, I'm afraid it's good news and bad news, so to speak."

Cecily studied the worried creases in Mrs. Chubb's face. "There's nothing wrong with the baby, is there?" she asked anxiously.

"No, mum. Not as far as I know, at any rate." Mrs. Chubb looked about the room in a distracted way, as if searching for the right words.

"Why don't you sit down, Altheda, and tell me what this is all about?" Her apprehension growing by leaps and bounds, Cecily moved to her chair at the head of the table and sat down herself, hoping to put the other woman more at ease.

Mrs. Chubb plopped herself down on a chair with a sigh. "It's Ian, mum," she said. "I'm very much afraid he's in bad trouble."

Remembering Samuel telling her that Ian had gone home earlier that day, Cecily frowned. "There's something wrong with him?"

"No . . . yes . . . Oh, dear lord."

Alarmed now, Cecily leaned forward. "Altheda, please say at once what it is you are trying to tell me."

"Well, mum, it's like this. When Ian and Gertie got married . . . Well, it seems that Ian already had a wife back in London."

Stunned, Cecily could only stare at her. "Ian? Already married?"

"Yes, mum. It seems that he got into trouble in the city and came down here to hide out. He went back every weekend until he got married to Gertie—that is, until she put her foot down. Well, his wife came looking for him, didn't she? And she found him in the end. Ian took her home with him and told Gertie the whole story."

"Oh, heavens. Then Gertie met the wife?"

"Yes, mum. She threw them out of the house."

"And where are they now?"

"Most likely on their way back to London, we reckon."

"Oh, poor child." Cecily rubbed her forehead. "Poor, poor Gertie. What a terrible shock. She must be absolutely devastated."

"Yes, mum, I think she is. She can't afford to stay in the cottage now, what with her earning only part-time and with Ian gone and all. With the baby coming, she's going to need somewhere to stay. I was wondering—"

"Where is Gertie now?" Cecily said, getting to her feet.

"She's in the kitchen. Michel's feeding her dinner, poor little mite. She being so upset about it all."

Cecily raised her eyebrows at this unexpected gesture from the volatile chef, but refrained from commenting on it. "Well, then, perhaps I should go and talk to her."

Mrs. Chubb sprang to her feet and hurried to the door. "She's very upset, mum, and you know Gertie when she gets upset, she's inclined to say things . . . er . . . She doesn't always watch her mouth—"

"Altheda," Cecily said firmly. "I have been known to curse myself at times."

Mrs. Chubb gasped. "You, mum? Oh, no, you are too much of a lady. You'd never utter the kind of language that Gertie uses."

"Maybe not out loud," Cecily said as she passed through the door and into the hallways, "but there have definitely been times when I have uttered the words under my breath." And right now, she added inwardly as she marched down the hallway, she'd very much like to say a few of them to Ian Rossiter.

On the way to the kitchen Mrs. Chubb filled her in on the

whole story. Cecily was startled to hear that his name wasn't Ian at all, but that he was in fact the mysterious Robert Johnson for whom the young woman was searching near the stables.

"I still can't believe it." Mrs. Chubb shook her head as they descended the stairs to the kitchen. "He was a bit of a brash lad and had a smart mouth at times, but I always thought he was a decent sort. I can't believe he would go and do something terrible like that. What in the world was he thinking of? Deserting his wife to marry another, when he had no right at all?"

"It is quite amazing what some people will do for the sake of love, Altheda," Cecily said, pausing at the kitchen door. "It is the most powerful emotion of all. And taken far too lightly at times, I'm afraid."

"That it is," Mrs. Chubb agreed as she pushed open the door. "That it is indeed."

The aroma of fried onions and bacon made Cecily's mouth water as she entered the warm, noisy kitchen. Michel stood by the stove, frying something in a huge pan that sizzled and spat when he shook it.

Gertie sat at the huge scrubbed-oak table, hungrily devouring a plate of liver and onions, piled high over a mound of mashed potatoes.

She jumped to her feet when she saw Cecily and bobbed a quick curtsy. "Good evening, mum," she mumbled and sent a nervous look at Mrs. Chubb.

"Don't talk with your mouth full, my girl," the house-keeper scolded.

"That's all right, Gertie," Cecily said as the girl chewed hurriedly and swallowed. "Just sit down there and finish your meal."

Michel turned from the stove, a large fork in his hand which he waved in the air like a wizard's wand. "You have come to sample the cooking, madame?"

Cecily smiled and shook her head. "No, Michel, I trust you implicitly. I know you will do your usual excellent job. I came to speak to Gertie."

The housemaid, who still stood by her chair looking as if

she was ready to bolt at any given moment, sent another desperate look at Mrs. Chubb.

"It's all right, Gertie," Cecily said, moving closer to the table. "Just sit down. Your dinner is growing cold."

Very slowly Gertie lowered herself onto the chair. She looked as if she were on the verge of bursting into tears, and Cecily's heart went out to her.

In an effort to relieve some of the young woman's anguish, she came straight to the point.

"Gertie, Mrs. Chubb has told me about your predicament. I want you to come back to your room at the Pennyfoot. You can work as much as your health allows until the baby is born, and then you may stay here for as long as you wish afterward. There will always be someone around to take care of the baby while you are working, and between us all I'm sure we can raise a healthy, happy child in this environment."

Gertie stared at her for several seconds, then laid her head on her arms and howled.

Michel shook his head and clicked his tongue. "Stop that caterwauling, *ma petite*, and finish your meal. I cannot create my masterpiece with that dreadful racket going on in my poor ears."

Mrs. Chubb clasped her hands, her face creased in smiles. "Oh, mum, just imagine. A baby in the house."

"Mon Dieu," Michel muttered, "my peace is forever shattered. Now I shall have to listen to a baby caterwauling as well as all these women."

Gertie stopped crying and lifted her head. "I'll keep it quiet, mum, I bleeding swear I will."

Mrs. Chubb groaned, but Cecily merely smiled. "Everything will work out well, I'm sure. Now dry your tears and finish your supper. I must get back upstairs."

"Oh, mum," Mrs. Chubb said quickly, "before you go, I wanted a word with you about Captain Phillips."

"Yes?" Cecily paused, wondering what else could possibly be wrong on this eventful day.

"Well, mum, he hadn't been down for his meals, not in three days, he hasn't. I sent Gertie up there to knock him up, and I sent meals up there, I've even been up there myself, but he doesn't want to open the door. He keeps telling us to leave him alone."

"He keeps telling us to bleeding drop dead, that's what he does," Gertie put in helpfully.

Mrs. Chubb threw her hands up in a gesture of defeat. "Well, in any case I am rather worried about him. His door is locked, of course, but I was wondering if perhaps Mr. Baxter could go up there with his set of keys and open the door. He might be ill, poor man, and is probably too embarrassed to ask for help."

"Yes, I agree," Cecily said, glancing at the clock over the stove. "But perhaps we should wait until after the dinner hour, just in case. If he hasn't come down tonight for dinner, I'll send Baxter upstairs with the keys."

"Thank you, mum," Mrs. Chubb said, obviously relieved. "It has been a worry, I can tell you. I shall be very happy to find out what is wrong up there."

"Well, let us hope it is nothing." Cecily turned to leave, then looked back at Mrs. Chubb. "By the way, is Ethel anywhere about?"

"She's in the dining room, mum, laying the tables."

"Well, as soon as she comes back, will you send her up to the library? I have a message I want her to deliver."

"I will do that right away, mum."

After thanking her, Cecily made her way back to the main floor. Soon the guests would be going down for dinner. By the time the meal was over, it would be quite dark. She should have plenty of time to put her plan into action. Now all she had to do was find Baxter and use her powers of persuasion on him one more time.

Baxter was not in his office when Cecily looked in there. After searching for him for a while, she learned he had gone into town on an errand and was not expected back for an hour. That would cut things considerably short, she thought worriedly, but there wasn't much she could do about it at that point. She would just have to pray that she would have enough time to accomplish what she had in mind.

She chose to eat in the dining room that evening and enjoyed a light meal before returning to the kitchen. Gertie still sat at the table and jumped guiltily to her feet when Cecily entered.

"I was just leaving, mum."

She still looked pale and considerably shaken, Cecily thought, studying the tear-stained face. With her dark hair and dark brown eyes, her pale skin showed up even more as a contrast.

Mrs. Chubb stood at the stove, cleaning up after Michel, who had apparently left for the day. She looked at Cecily, an anxious expression on her face. "Is he all right, mum?"

For a moment Cecily was confused. "Who?"

"Captain Phillips. I thought Mr. Baxter might have gone up by now to see what's the matter."

"Oh, no, Baxter is in town," Cecily said, her gaze returning to the housemaid, who had gathered up her shawl and wound it around her shoulders. "Gertie, I really do feel you should stay here tonight. It won't be very pleasant for you to return to the empty cottage at this hour."

Gertie's lip trembled, but she managed to keep the tears at bay. "No, mum, it bleeding won't. That's very kind of you, I'm sure."

"I'll see that a bed is made up for her," Mrs. Chubb said briskly. "A good night's sleep will do wonders for the miseries, you'll see."

Gertie didn't look too convinced, but she managed a smile. "I bloody hope so," she said, sounding a little stronger.

"I noticed that Captain Phillips was not in the dining room, Altheda," Cecily said while Gertie took off her shawl again. "Since Baxter won't be back for a while, I have collected the master keys. I'd like you to come with me to the top floor now, and we will find out what is wrong up there."

The housekeeper dropped the spoon she was holding with a clatter. "Oh, madam, don't you think it would be better if we waited for Mr. Baxter? Heaven knows what we'll find up there. What if the captain has taken ill and becomes violent? Some people do that when they are delirious, you know.''

"I hardly think that the captain would have answered you in the manner that he did if he'd been delirious," Cecily said firmly. "In any case, we must know if the poor man needs help. We can't just let him lie there and suffer.''

Mrs. Chubb reached for the spoon and placed it with the others in the pot of hot water. "Yes, mum. Of course I'll come with you, then.''

"Can I come?" Gertie said, her face brightening just a shade. "I'd like to know what's wrong with the old geezer. He ain't a bad sort really. In any case, you might need help. Three pairs of flipping hands will be better than two, won't they?''

"Oh, I don't think—" Mrs. Chubb began, but Cecily forestalled her.

"I think that's an excellent idea. Although I am quite sure we are in no danger from Captain Phillips, it will be reassuring to have reinforcements, should they be needed.''

Mrs. Chubb eyed Gertie's husky build. "Good idea. Do you think perhaps we should take something up with us, mum? Just in case? A knife or something?''

Cecily looked at her in alarm. "Heavens, no. We don't want to scare the poor man out of his wits. I'm quite sure there is a simple explanation for all this. Perhaps the captain just decided to fast for some reason. Or more than likely he has some illness that has robbed him of his appetite. In any case, we should go up there now and solve the matter.''

"Very well." Mrs. Chubb dusted her hands together as if she were preparing herself for a boxing match. "You ready, then, Gertie?''

Gertie's face now wore a fierce scowl. "You'd better believe I'm bleeding ready. And just let him try any funny tricks, that's all. The bloody mood I'm in, I'll wipe the blinking floor with him, I will.''

"I sincerely hope that won't be necessary," Cecily said as she led them out of the kitchen. "Though I do wish Baxter had been here to take care of this for us.''

"We could wait for him," Mrs. Chubb said as they

reached the foyer. "One more hour isn't going to make that much difference, is it?"

Cecily shook her head. "I have an important matter to take care of, and I want to leave as soon as Baxter returns. I'll need him to come with me, and he wouldn't have time to take care of the captain until much later. I think it best we deal with it now, so that if we have to send for Dr. Prestwick right away we can do so. I do hate to knock the poor man up in the middle of the night."

"Oh, yes, mum," Mrs. Chubb said, beginning to puff as they climbed the first flight of stairs. "Especially a man like Dr. Prestwick. He works so hard all day in his surgery, then all evening calling on people. And if there's a baby born, you can be sure it will be in the middle of the night."

Gertie made a small sound, and Mrs. Chubb patted her on the arm. "Don't you worry, ducks. You'll be here, won't you? Surrounded by people whom you know. Just think, if Ian hadn't left, you would have been all alone in the cottage to have that baby."

"Yeah," Gertie said mournfully. "I suppose that's something."

"Always a silver lining, ducks," Mrs. Chubb said, panting between the words. "All you have to do is look for it." The keys hanging from the housekeeper's belt bumped and jangled against her hip as the three of them mounted the stairs.

The room keys that Cecily carried chimed in harmony. They sounded like jailors doing the rounds of the prisons, she thought, half smiling at the idea. Not that she felt much like smiling. Heaven knew what awaited them at the top of the stairs, and she still had the night's ordeal to get through afterward.

She could only hope that Baxter would agree to help her. Not that he'd ever refused before. But she knew only too well that each time she dragged him into one of her escapades, his patience became a little more ragged.

She had no choice, however. It was the only way she could think of to prove who had murdered Lady Sherbourne.

They reached the top landing and waited while Mrs.

Chubb got her breath back. Cecily jingled the keys restlessly in her hand, her nerves tightening as the thought of what might lie down the shadowy corridor.

Leading the way, she moved slowly toward the captain's room. She paused outside the door, holding up her hand for everyone to be quiet, though neither Mrs. Chubb nor Gertie seemed able to breathe properly, let alone speak.

Cecily laid her ear against the door, but she could hear nothing other than the hiss of the gas lamps and the quick, short breaths of the two women with her.

Impatient with her reluctance to act, she lifted her hand and rapped loudly on the door.

Mrs. Chubb uttered a faint "Oooh" and pressed both hands against her bosom. Gertie just stood there, her eyes as big and round as the full moon.

"Captain Phillips," Cecily said as brusquely as she knew how. "This is Cecily Sinclair. I really must insist that you open this door at once so that we may give you whatever assistance you might need."

"Watcha want?" a weary voice answered.

"Oh, gawd, he's got to be bad," Gertie whispered. "His voice ain't half faint."

"It is a lot weaker than it was," Mrs. Chubb agreed.

Again Cecily rapped on the door. "Captain? If you do not open this door on the count of five, I shall open it myself and come in there." She rattled the keys for good measure, hoping he would realize she was prepared to carry out her threat.

"Drop bleeding dead," the captain answered.

"See?" Gertie hissed. "That's what he always says."

Her patience exhausted, Cecily took one of the keys and fitted it into the lock. She tried to turn it, but nothing happened, and she had to select three more and test them before the lock turned smoothly with a loud click.

Once more she tried to get a response from the sea captain. "I have the door unlocked," she announced, "and I will count to five. Then I will open the door."

From inside the room came a faint muttering, too low for the women outside to understand.

"Very well," Cecily said, wishing fervently that Baxter was standing next to her. "One, two, three, four . . ." She hesitated.

"Five!" Gertie said loudly, making them all jump.

"Gertie!" Mrs. Chubb turned a fierce scowl on her.

"Sorry, got bleeding carried away," the housemaid muttered.

Cecily squared her shoulders and took hold of the handle. Very slowly she pushed open the door.

"Bloody hell," Gertie said.

There on the floor in front of them, the lifeless figure of the captain lay flat on his back. It didn't take a close examination to ensure the captain was dead. The smell was so powerful for a moment that Cecily thought she would be sick.

She held the doorjamb to steady herself as her head swam dizzily. Then her vision cleared again, and she raised her gaze to the birdcage that sat in the middle of the room.

Inside the cage a very large, very dejected-looking green parrot gazed back at them. As she watched, it stretched its claws, then its neck.

"Drop bleeding dead," it said mournfully.

CHAPTER
✠18✠

"I do wish you would tell me why we are skulking around in the woods at this unearthly hour of the night," Baxter said in a hoarse whisper. "I cannot for the life of me imagine why I allowed you to persuade me to accompany you on this ridiculous venture."

"You came," Cecily reminded him, "because you knew quite well that I would come alone if you refused to accompany me."

"Shush," Baxter hissed urgently. "Voices carry in the dark, you know."

Cecily peered around the gnarled trunk of a thick oak tree to where the maypole stood in solitary splendor in the center of the Downs. Although it was several yards away, the moon illuminated the grassy slopes, and she could see the ribbons quite clearly swaying in the night breeze.

"I do think we shall hear him coming long before he hears us," she said mildly. She did, however, lower her voice.

"Hear who?" Baxter muttered.

Cecily didn't answer. In the distance she could hear the faint wash of water on the sand, and above her head the wind rustling the branches. She thought she had heard something else as well, but she couldn't be sure.

"Hear who?" Baxter repeated irritably.

He had put his mouth close to her ear, to make himself heard more clearly without raising his voice.

She jumped violently, her nerves already strung out as tight as a corset string. "Oh, do be quiet, Baxter," she muttered. "You sound like an owl."

"I beg your pardon, madam."

Aware that she'd offended him, she peered up at him in the shadowy darkness. "I'm sorry," she whispered. "I was trying to hear."

"Hear—" He snapped his mouth shut.

She felt an inane desire to laugh. Controlling herself, she said softly, "I thought I heard hoofbeats."

"Surely you are not expecting to see whatever it was that imbecile Fortescue was blabbering about the other night?"

"No, I am not. I am, however, expecting to see whoever it was who murdered Lady Sherbourne."

"So you said earlier. You have yet to enlighten me as to the villain's identity, however."

"That's because I am not sure of his identity." Cecily looked back across the Downs. Nothing moved out there except for the ribbons on the maypole, swaying gently in the night wind from the sea.

A cloud slid across the moon, casting a deep, wide shadow to race over the rough grass. Cecily held her breath until the cloud moved on, allowing the moonlight to glow once more.

"You are not sure of his identity?" Baxter echoed. "Then how do you know he will be here?"

"I don't." They had been talking in whispers, and Cecily was becoming tired of it. Allowing her voice to filter through softly, she said, "I am merely hoping that he will."

"If you ask me," Baxter said, forgetting to whisper also, "this entire escapade is nothing but a waste of time. I should be back at the hotel, waiting for Dr. Prestwick to arrive to tend to that poor man lying upstairs."

"I don't think much can be done for him now," Cecily said, shuddering at the memory. "He was quite dead."

"At least it appears he died a natural death. I could see no wounds on his body."

"I don't know how you could get that close to tell. The smell was quite appalling."

"I wanted to reassure myself before I left him there for the doctor." Baxter sighed. "I feel quite badly about the poor man. I should not have left him there alone."

"Captain Phillips won't be feeling any discomfort," Cecily said, glancing up at him again. "And he certainly won't be going anywhere."

"I was referring to the doctor," Baxter said stiffly, "and I really don't feel in the mood for levity."

He stuck his hands into his trousers pockets, a gesture she found quite amazing. For once Baxter was not standing on ceremony in her presence. She could count on the toes of one foot how many times he had displayed such a lapse, and always when he was under a great deal of stress.

"I'm sorry, Baxter, I do not mean to be flippant. We could be here for quite a while before anything happens. I was merely attempting to alleviate the tension, that's all."

"If I might be permitted to say so, madam, the most successful way to alleviate the stress would be to return to the hotel and leave all this cloak-and-dagger nonsense to the police, who are, after all, trained in such matters."

"Why, Baxter, how very generous of you, considering how you feel about our local constabulary."

"Hmmmph," Baxter muttered, rather rudely, Cecily thought. He must be feeling even more tense than usual.

She looked back across the Downs again, straining her ears to catch the slightest sound, but all she heard was the gentle swish of the waves and the wind softly sighing through the oak trees.

Trying to think of a way to break the strained silence

between them, she said quietly, "Baxter, tell me why you have taken such a dislike to Stan Northcott."

"I prefer not to discuss the matter, madam."

She looked up at him and saw his gaze glinting down at her. "I know he's not the most intelligent of men, but neither is he a fool," she insisted. "I feel, somehow, that he has mistreated you in some way in the past, and for some reason you can't forgive him."

It wasn't too dark to see his eyebrows lift. "You are very perceptive, madam."

She smiled. "Sometimes it helps to talk about it."

"Not at this time, I think."

Frustrated now, she became even more determined to learn the answer to a question that had puzzled her for a very long time. "Baxter, I am your friend, am I not?"

He stretched his chin, as he always did when embarrassed. "Yes, madam. I would agree with that."

"And it is customary to take one's friends into one's confidences."

"At times, perhaps."

"I should be most hurt if I felt that you did not trust me enough as a friend to know that I would understand anything you might care to tell me."

"Madam, with all due respect, this is a matter I prefer to keep to myself."

"Piffle, Baxter. You are just being stubborn."

She glared up at him, and he scowled back. They stayed this way for several seconds, then Baxter let out his breath in an explosive burst.

"If I may say so, madam, you can be extremely exasperating at times."

Cecily smiled grimly. "James often said the same thing."

"And I can sympathize with your husband's dilemma. I fear I would not have had his patience in dealing with such aggravation."

"Really, Bax?" Cecily said sweetly. "And just how would you have dealt with me?"

She could tell by the way he ran a finger around his collar that his face had heated.

"That is not for me to say, madam," he said a trifle hoarsely.

"You disappoint me, my friend." She turned away from him, unwilling to let him see how he had affected her.

To her utter surprise, Baxter said quietly, "P.C. Northcott and I were once rivals for the same young lady."

She swung her head up sharply. "You and Stan? But he must be ten years younger than you."

Baxter cleared his throat. "Yes, madam. So was the young lady."

"Oh." Cecily studied this news in silence. She had often wondered why Baxter had never married. He was an attractive man. Even now, at the age of forty-one, his solid frame bore little fat, and his hair was still dark, except for patches of gray at the temples.

While she had more than her fair share of gray in her light brown hair, and she was no more than two years older than her manager.

"You knew him in Wellercombe, then. Wasn't that where he served his first few years?"

"Yes, madam. I worked in a hotel not too far from the police station."

"So tell me what happened," she said, anxious now to hear the details.

"Madam," Baxter protested. "I really don't think—"

"Why don't you ever address me by my first name?"

He seemed unable to answer her for a moment, then he said faintly, "It is not my place, madam."

She longed to tell him he was wrong. If only he wasn't so bound by the proprieties that governed his life. But she would never change him. Even if their positions were to be magically reversed in some way, he would never be able to forget that she was once the wife of the man who had employed him, and that she was now his employer.

"This young lady chose Stan over you?" she said, regretfully changing the subject again.

At first, she thought he had chosen not to answer, then he said softly, "He stole her away from me."

Cecily felt a stab of envy for this woman who had once had Baxter's love. "Then the woman was a fool."

Baxter shook his head. "I was too old for her. Set in my ways. In those days Stan Northcott was a brash young policeman, full of energy and his own sense of importance. He must have appeared very dashing to my . . . to the young lady."

Cecily thought about the dumpy, almost lethargic constable she had known for several years. It was difficult to see him as dashing, particularly in comparison with Baxter.

Then again, Baxter could be quite pompous at times, unless one knew how to disarm him. "Would that be the same woman who is now Stan's wife?" she asked, intrigued to have discovered a side of Baxter she had never imagined.

"No." He paused, and she waited, seeing his dark head silhouetted against the night sky, his expression hidden from her by the shadows. "Northcott lost interest in her once he had won her love. He callously cast her aside for the woman who is now his wife."

"Oh." She was almost afraid to ask, sensing a tragedy behind the even tone of his voice. Yet she wanted desperately to know. "What happened to her?"

"She took her own life, madam. I understand she was bearing his child at the time."

She felt a lump in her throat and knew she couldn't utter the words that hovered there. She reached out a hand to touch his arm, then froze when she heard the faint sound in the distance.

From out of the darkness came the distinct vibration of hoofbeats thudding across the grass.

Cecily saw Baxter straighten his body abruptly and felt her own nerves tense. Looking back across the Downs, she waited, her heart beating wildly, for the horseman to appear.

Closer and closer came the hoofbeats, louder and louder until the thunder of them echoed through the trees. Suddenly the horse and rider burst into view.

In spite of her own reassurances to herself, Cecily felt

almost a sense of anticlimax as the horse cantered up to the maypole and came to a snorting, pawing halt. She could see the silhouette of the rider quite clearly. He had a perfectly good head sitting on his shoulders.

"You have everything ready?" Cecily whispered, although she already knew the answer.

"Yes, madam." The words were barely audible.

She nodded. "Then here we go."

She took a step forward and felt strong fingers grip her arm.

"Please take care . . . madam."

She smiled at him in the darkness, and he let her go. Taking a deep breath, she stepped out of the shadows of the woods and into the clear moonlight.

The rider watched her as she approached, his hands on the reins to control his steed, who sidestepped back and forth, tossing his head and snorting through his nostrils.

The clear, white light from the moon enabled her to see Lord Sherbourne's face quite clearly as she moved closer.

He did not appear to be surprised at her appearance. "Mrs. Sinclair," he said, making no attempt to soften his deep voice. "Something told me I would find you here. When I read your note, supposedly written by a gypsy who had seen me murder my wife and who was demanding a price for my silence, I had to question the immaculate prose."

"My mistake," Cecily said evenly. "I should have given that more thought."

The horse moved sideways a few steps, and Lord Sherbourne guided it back to the spot. "Indeed you should have. Am I to understand that it is yourself who is demanding such a price for your silence? You must be in dire need of money to take such a risk."

"I do not believe that you will risk killing twice in the same place." Cecily pulled her shawl closer about her shoulders as the wind chilled her neck. "I am in desperate need of funds for the hotel. For that I would risk a great deal."

Radley stared down at her for a long moment. "What kind

of guarantee would you offer that you will keep your silence once I have paid for it?"

"You have my word, sir."

Radley threw back his head and laughed. "And I am to accept that?"

"I do not believe you have much choice in the matter. If you do not pay me, I shall be forced to go to the police and tell them what I know."

"And what do you know, Mrs. Sinclair?" Radley leaned low across the horse's neck to peer down at her. "I doubt very much that you were anywhere near this place when Barbara was murdered. You are playing a guessing game, madam. An extremely dangerous one, I might add."

Cecily clenched her hands but otherwise showed no sign of apprehension. "I know that you killed your wife, sir. I know that you lured her up here on the Downs, after telling your brother that she planned to go shopping with Lady Deirdre. While alone with her, you strangled her with one of the maypole ribbons."

"Really?" Radley's laugh was silky smooth. "Perhaps you'd be so kind as to enlighten me as to why I should wish to destroy the only person who has ever brought light and joy to my life."

"That I cannot say," Cecily said reluctantly. "But if I were to guess, I would say it has something to do with her interest in your brother Sylvester."

He sat up so suddenly the horse reared. Cursing, he controlled it, then looked down at her again. The mocking expression had vanished from his face, leaving a vicious scowl that caused Cecily to wonder why she had ever thought him handsome.

"I see you have been quite busy poking your nasty little nose into my family's business," he said harshly. "That was a very bad mistake, madam. And I can assure you your assumptions are nothing more than wisps of smoke. One strong puff and they will disappear."

"You also made a mistake, sir," Cecily said, refusing to back away when he brought the horse closer to her.

"I don't make mistakes."

"You apparently had forgotten your alibi when you asked
Lady Deirdre to purchase your snuff while in town. Had you
known that your wife was to accompany her, it surely would
have been far more suitable to have asked her to buy it for
you."

"Is that all?" Once more his mocking laugh rang out. "My
wife wasn't available to ask at the time. My sister-in-law
happened to be there when I realized I was out of snuff, and
I asked her to purchase some for me."

"Really? Then how was it you didn't mention to Lady
Deirdre at that time that your wife planned to go shopping
with her? You had already mentioned the fact to your
brother Arthur."

"Perhaps I forgot."

This time Cecily smiled. "I think not. Besides, none of
that matters when it is proved that it was your snuffbox
found this morning lying at the edge of the woods."

"All conjecture, my dear lady."

She could see, however, that she had made him nervous.
Radley stared at her thoughtfully for several moments. "But
I admit you could be a great nuisance to me if you insisted
on tattling this nonsense to the police. I do, however,
heartily detest blackmailers."

"Is that why you killed your wife, Lord Sherbourne?"
Cecily asked boldly.

He sat for another long space of time before saying
quietly, "As a matter of fact, it was. I found out, quite by
chance, she was blackmailing my brother Sylvester. I found
some very expensive jewelry that I had not purchased
myself, and which had not been paid for out of my accounts.

"After a little more investigating, I discovered that
Sylvester had withdrawn a large amount of cash recently. I
put two and two together. Knowing my wife and my brother,
it was not that difficult to do. They had an affair, Sylvester
eventually tired of her, and she threatened to tell me unless
he paid her handsomely for her silence."

"So you brought her up here to murder her?"

He uttered a long sigh. "No," he said, sounding almost
regretful. "I learned that Sylvester had an appointment at

the bank in town that afternoon, presumably to withdraw more money to keep my wife's mouth shut. I brought her up here that afternoon to have it out with her. I expected the exchange to be heated. I wanted to be rid of her. It was bad enough that she had deceived me, but to betray me with my own brother, that I could never forgive."

Once more the horse moved restlessly. "I needed to be somewhere where we wouldn't be overheard," he continued when he'd settled the animal again. "I intended to protect the family's reputation at all costs."

He tilted his head back for a moment to look at the sky, then lowered his face again. "I told Arthur that my wife intended to go shopping, because I didn't want the fool trailing after us. He was quite besotted by her, you know. Followed her everywhere. It's ironic, actually. Barbara was infatuated with the wrong brother. Arthur would have been delighted to return her affection."

"So you told her what you knew?" Cecily prompted, anxious not to be done with the whole confession.

"I offered her a large sum of money if she would leave us in peace and never return. I had hoped to avoid a scandal in the family. It was of my utmost concern. After a while, I would quietly divorce her."

Cecily could well imagine how Lady Sherbourne had received that suggestion. "She refused," she said softly.

"Not only did she refuse, she made a mockery of me. She danced around that damn maypole, taunting me, insulting me, until I finally lost my temper."

"And you strangled her."

"I didn't intend to. I wanted to frighten her into submission. She struggled, and before I knew it, she was dead."

Cecily wasn't too sure she believed that, but it no longer mattered. It was enough to know that he confessed to killing his wife.

"I returned at once to the hotel," Radley went on, "and spent the rest of the afternoon in my suite, trying to decide what to do. Then it occurred to me that no one knew I had been here with Barbara. I decided to keep quiet. After all, the family name was at stake. Had I confessed, the entire scandal would have been brought to light."

Cecily frowned. "But you returned to the Downs later that night, did you not?"

He looked down at her. "How did you know that?"

"Colonel Fortescue. I believe it was you who leaped over him on your horse that night."

"That fool. I didn't think anyone would listen to anything he said. I came back that night to make sure Barbara was dead. The thought that she might not be haunted me all afternoon. I didn't see the colonel until I was almost on top of him. I covered my head with my cape so that he wouldn't recognize me."

"He didn't," Cecily assured him. "But when he mentioned the cape, I knew it had to be you."

The horse sidestepped again as Radley pulled up on the reins. "I must admit you have been most clever. But there is only one way to deal with blackmailers, Mrs. Sinclair. My wife paid for her sins, and now, I'm afraid, so shall you. I refuse to buy your silence, but after everything I have done to preserve the family name, I cannot allow you to besmirch it now." He swung a leg over the saddle and leaped lightly to the ground.

Cecily took a hasty step backward and stumbled over the hem of her skirt. She caught her balance and stood facing the man standing silently in front of her. "I don't think it would be wise of you to commit the same crime twice," she said sharply, raising her voice.

"Oh, indeed I shall, my dear lady. You will die in exactly the same manner as my wife. It will be a simple matter to strap you to the pole and then tighten a ribbon around your neck. You will be dead in seconds. The police will merely assume that it is the work of the gypsies again."

Cecily raised a hand to her throat. "Then you did intentionally murder your wife," she said, her voice ringing out across the lonely Downs.

"Yes, I did." His words trembled with rage. "I lost my temper. I wanted to squeeze every last breath from her body. I wanted to make sure that no one ever touched her again.

And I did. I destroyed her, just as she destroyed me. And now, madam, you, too, will know the folly of attempting to extort a member of the Boscombe family."

He took a step toward her, then halted, his eyes wide and staring at something behind her.

Cecily swung around. Advancing toward her was a line of fire, a row of flaming torches held in the hands of swarthy-faced men. Shoulder to shoulder they approached, their expression grim in the reflection of the dancing flames.

At the head of the line Baxter marched steadily forward, striding side by side with a thickset man who wore a bandanna wound about his forehead.

For several seconds it seemed as if both Cecily and Radley were transfixed by the sight. Then the line halted. In the silence that followed, Cecily became acutely aware of the waves splashing on the sands below and the impatient snorting of the restless stallion.

Then even those sounds seemed to fade as the leader of the gypsies slowly raised his hand.

CHAPTER
❖19❖

The rasping voice of the gypsy leader rang out loud and clear across the rolling slopes of the Downs.

"Lord Sherbourne," the leader declared solemnly, "we are here to seek retribution. You have brought suspicion and shame on the gypsy tribes and have caused us unnecessary discomfort and tribulation. Because of your crime, and your failure to accept the consequences, we have suffered severe harassment from the police and are now forced to leave our home and find a new dwelling elsewhere."

A low muttering began to spread down the line as the gypsies' faces turned hostile. Several of them brandished their torches, sending sparks flying in the wind, bright against the night sky.

Lord Sherbourne started to say something, but the gypsy leader silenced him by again holding up his hand. "You have been judged and found guilty, Lord Sherbourne. The gypsies do not follow the law of the land. We have our own law, and we deal out justice in our own way."

The voices became louder, more belligerent, muttering curses and threats as the men again brandished the torches. Then slowly, side by side, they continued to advance.

With a low curse Radley leaped for the horse. In the same instant the gypsies, apparently scenting his possible escape, charged forward, their torches streaming sparks as they yelled for blood.

The horse whinnied, and Cecily stumbled out of the way as it plunged past her, the white of its eye rolling in terror.

Radley shouted something and hauled on the reins, to no avail. The horse had its head, and it wasn't about to stop. Pursued by the yelling gypsies and their flaming torches, the terrified animal headed straight for the cliffs.

Her hand at her throat, Cecily watched as Radley attempted at the very last minute to fling himself from the stallion's broad back. He'd left it too late. Even as he swung his leg across the saddle, the horse plunged off the steep cliff, its shrieks mingling with the deathly howl of the man clinging to its neck. Then came an almighty splash. And silence.

The row of men halted just a few feet from where Cecily stood. Baxter strode swiftly to her side, his face a mask of concern.

"You are not hurt?" he asked urgently.

She shook her head. "I suppose there is no point in attempting a rescue?"

"I very much doubt it." He offered her his arm. "Come with me, I'll take you back to the trap. You can wait for me there while I talk to these chaps. I won't keep you waiting too long."

Gratefully she took hold of his arm and let him lead her back through the woods to where they had left the chestnut tied to a tree.

She felt immeasurably weary for some reason, and it was a great effort to climb up into the seat.

"You will be all right here until I return?" Baxter asked her, his face drawn tight with anxiety.

"I will be just fine, Baxter. I will just rest here until you have spoken with the men."

"Very well, madam. I will be but a few short minutes."

She nodded and closed her eyes. It had been a long day, and for once her energy had deserted her. Perhaps she was growing too old for all this excitement and adventure, she reflected, then scolded herself for such weakness. She just needed a short rest, and she would be back to her old self in no time.

In spite of the jumbled thoughts tumbling through her mind, she must have dozed, for she awoke with a start to hear Baxter's voice.

"Madam? Cecily? Are you not feeling well?"

She opened her eyes and saw his anxious gaze on her face. "You actually called me by my first name," she said sleepily.

"I did?" He cleared his throat. "I did. I beg your pardon, madam. It won't happen again."

"Piffle, Bax," she mumbled, huddling down further onto the seat. "I liked it." Only half aware of him climbing aboard the driver's seat, she pulled her shawl around her shoulders.

The fresh sea breeze revived her as the trap jiggled and creaked back to the hotel, and when Baxter helped her down from her seat, she was able to smile at him with that usual animation.

"I wonder if Dr. Prestwick has called in to examine the captain's body. If he did then he must have left again, since his trap isn't here."

"At this late hour I should imagine he is at home in bed," Baxter said, moving ahead of her to open the door.

"That sounds like a very good idea." She walked past him into the foyer, grateful for the warmth after the cool night air. "I think I will retire for the night myself."

"I think that would be wise. Can I make you a pot of tea first?"

"Thank you, no." She looked up at him, noticing for the first time his wind-ruffled hair. It made him look quite human, for once. And very appealing. "You will have to see to the horse and trap, I'm afraid. Now that Ian has gone, we shall have to find someone else to work with Samuel in the stables."

Baxter looked shocked. "Ian has gone? Gone where?"

Cecily sighed. "I'm sorry, Baxter, I forgot you didn't know. In all the excitement of this evening's events, the matter went right out of my head."

"This was quite sudden, wasn't it? Why didn't he have the decency to inform me he was leaving?" Baxter frowned. "Why did not anyone inform me of his departure?"

"Would you mind if we discussed this matter in the morning? I really am dreadfully tired." She smiled up at him in appeal. "I will tell you the entire story tomorrow, and then we can start searching for a replacement."

He still looked put out but said quietly, "Very well, madam, I will attend to the matter as soon as possible."

"Thank you, Baxter." She turned to leave, then looked back at him. "Lord Sherbourne was dead, I suppose?"

"Yes, madam. It was most fortunate that the men agreed to your plan. Otherwise it could well have been you or me lying crushed to death on those rocks."

"I have to confess, the men were a wonderful sight to behold. He intended to hang me on the maypole. He might well have done it had it not been for that line of gypsies." Cecily felt a slight shudder.

"But then I should have rushed to your rescue," Baxter declared.

She gave him a tired smile. "You would? How very gallant of you, Baxter."

"I have my doubts as to how successful I might have been. Without the help of the gypsies, I am not sure I could have dealt with the man single-handedly. He had a powerful build and was very fast on his feet."

"So are you, Baxter. I'm quite sure you would have trounced the man in no time."

He looked inordinately pleased. "Thank you, madam."

"Not at all, Baxter."

"The gypsies agreed to recover the body and were attempting that as I left. They will be taking him to the police station and will inform the inspector of his confession. It will then be up to the police if they wish to pursue the matter."

Cecily smothered a yawn. "Oh, dear me, do excuse me. I really don't think they will pursue the matter, Baxter. I am sure that since Lord Sherbourne has paid dearly for his sins, there will be no point in causing a scandal for the rest of the family. Inspector Cranshaw is most reluctant to offend the aristocracy unless absolutely necessary."

"As I am well aware, madam. I am quite sure the death will be attributed to an accident, thereby concealing any part played by you in this entire situation. It would seem that fortune has smiled upon you once more."

"Yes, I do believe you are right. A fitting end to a most interesting adventure."

"You will not always be so fortunate, madam. If you persist in this reckless behavior, there is bound to come a time when you will find yourself in hot water and unable to get out."

Cecily sighed. "You may be right, Baxter. But right now I really am too weary to worry about it. I will say good night, and we will discuss this further in the morning."

"Yes, madam."

She looked up at him, trying to fight the sudden depression that seemed to have settled like a cloak about her shoulders. "Thank you, Baxter, for being there with me tonight. As always, I found your presence indispensable."

"It was nothing, madam. I am happy that everything transpired so well, if a trifle unexpected."

"Yes, I must admit that was not the way I had planned for it to end. I don't know whether to be sorry or relieved that the matter was taken out of our hands."

"Count your blessings," Baxter murmured. "And accept the divine will."

"I do, Baxter, I certainly do." She hitched up her skirt to begin climbing the stairs. "I will bid you good night, then."

"Good night, madam."

She didn't know why she should feel so sad. For a moment or two out there on the windswept Downs, she had felt an affinity with Baxter that she had never experienced before. And now, inside the walls of the hotel once more, she appeared to have lost it again.

Mounting the stairs, one by one, she couldn't help wondering if she would ever reach the kind of intimacy she would like to share with him. Then she smiled, thinking how shocked and embarrassed he would be by her thoughts.

The next morning she arose feeling refreshed, her depression having been lightened by a deep sleep. Shortly after breakfast Ethel informed her that the inspector waited for her in the library, and after summoning Baxter, Cecily hurried down the hallway to face the reticent gentleman.

He stood with his back to the French windows, hands clasped behind him, his usual morose expression on his angular face. Standing next to him, the short, stubby P.C. Northcott with his florid complexion and bushy mustache looked almost clownish by comparison.

Cecily greeted them both, then took her customary seat at the table. She had to sit sideways in order to face the inspector, who showed no inclination to move. Stan Northcott hovered somewhere around midpoint.

Looking at him, Cecily was reminded of Baxter's confidences the night before. She simply could not imagine the constable as ever being considered dashing.

"Mrs. Sinclair," Cranshaw began in his clipped voice, "I have some tragic news to import. I am afraid another of your guests has met with an accident."

"Oh?" Cecily did her best to look shocked and distressed. "Which one of my guests? Is it serious?"

"Quite serious I'm afraid. Lord Sherbourne was riding on the Downs late last night when apparently his horse was startled by something. It appears that the horse bolted and fell over the cliff."

"Oh, my." Cecily clutched her throat in a dramatic fashion. "I imagine the poor thing was killed."

The inspector narrowed his gaze. After a moment he said quietly, "A fall from that height, madam, would hardly facilitate the animal's good health."

Northcott snickered, which earned a scowl of reproof from his superior. The constable's grin vanished.

"No, quite," Cecily murmured. "But what of Lord Sherbourne?"

"I regret to inform you, madam, that he also perished. A most unfortunate accident."

"Oh, goodness." Remembering the sight and sounds of animal and rider hurtling to their death was enough to add credence to Cecily's expression of horror. "That poor family. Another tragedy so soon. They must be simply devastated. Have they been informed?"

"Yes, madam. I informed them myself thirty minutes ago."

She gave the inspector a look full of innocence. "Do you suppose, Inspector, that the poor man, stricken with grief over the unfortunate death of his wife, decided to join her in the hereafter?"

Cranshaw met her gaze with cool detachment. "I prefer to believe, madam, that His Lordship's death happened as I described. For the sake of the family's good name, and in view of their suffering, I suggest you eliminate that theory from your mind."

"Of course, Inspector. I wouldn't dream of repeating it outside the walls of this room."

He stared at her, as if not sure what to make of that remark. Fortunately at that moment the door opened to admit Baxter, who looked a trifle put out to discover the proceedings had begun without him.

His questioning gaze went straight to Cecily, who returned it with a calm smile. It didn't appear to reassure him, and he shot an anxious glance at the inspector. "You sent for me, madam?" he said, addressing Cecily with a slight bow of his head.

"Baxter, I'm afraid the inspector has some most distressing news. Please inform my manager, if you would, Inspector, of the events of last night."

The inspector repeated the news, while she sat back, enjoying Baxter's attempts to look suitably shaken. That he was extremely nervous was obvious to her. She hoped it wasn't quite so apparent to Cranshaw. The constable merely stood there, a vacant expression on his face.

More than likely he was trying to think of a way to pay the kitchen a quick visit on his way out, Cecily thought, eyeing him with less approval than she once afforded him. After the way he had treated the woman Baxter had loved, she would never feel quite the same about him again.

Again she felt that faint stirring of emotion at the thought of Baxter being in love with another woman. Jealousy, she realized with a shock. She was actually jealous of an unfortunate, unknown woman who had died many years ago. How terribly immature of her.

She became aware of a silence in the room and looked up to find Baxter watching her, a slight frown on his face. She realized Cranshaw had asked her a question, and she hurriedly redirected her gaze. "I am sorry, Inspector, my thoughts were elsewhere for the moment. May I ask what it was you wanted to know?"

"I asked if you were not aware that Lord Sherbourne had not returned last night," Cranshaw said, his keen gaze probing her face.

Cecily cast her mind back, wondering if anything she'd said had pointed to the fact that she already knew of Radley's death. Or maybe Cranshaw was simply suspicious because of her previous involvement in some of his recent cases.

"My mind was concerned last night with the death of Captain Phillips," she said quite truthfully. She glanced back at Baxter as a thought occurred to her. "Did Dr. Prestwick make his call here last night?"

Cranshaw confirmed her speculation by answering, "Dr. Prestwick reported to me first thing this morning. He informed me that Captain Phillips died of a heart attack approximately three days ago."

"Ah," Cecily said smoothly, hoping she was wrong about her concern. "Then it was the voice of the parrot my staff heard when they attempted to speak to the captain."

"Yes, madam. Dr. Prestwick also informed me that he inquired as to your presence while he was here. He was informed that you and Mr. Baxter were not in the hotel, which rather surprised him, considering the late hour."

Having already suspected as much, Cecily was prepared. "Baxter and myself were taking care of a domestic matter. One of my staff left rather suddenly, deserting his pregnant wife who was in great need of consolation and reassurance."

Not really a lie, she assured herself, more a twisting around of the truth. She dared not catch Baxter's eye, for she could guess his expression. Instead, she kept her gaze steadily on the inspector's skeptical face.

"I see," he said slowly, as if he did indeed see through her fabrication and had decided not to challenge it.

Apparently growing impatient, P.C. Northcott cleared his throat loudly, then coughed.

To Cecily's relief, the inspector took the cue. "Very well, Mrs. Sinclair, I won't take up any more of your time. In view of the latest developments, we have decided to discontinue our investigation of Lady Sherbourne's murder and will record it as death at the hands of a person or persons unknown."

"Thank you, Inspector. I am sure that will be a relief to the members of the Boscombe family. I assume they are now free to leave?"

"Yes, as a matter of fact, I believe they are making preparations to do so now." Cranshaw moved swiftly across the floor while the constable made a clumsy lunge for the door, almost knocking Baxter off his feet.

Baxter sent him a look of utter disdain, which was entirely lost on Northcott as he fumbled the door open and stood back to let Cranshaw pass through.

The inspector paused in the doorway and looked back at Cecily. "I have also lifted the quarantine on the murder site. So the May Day festivities can take place as usual."

"Thank you, Inspector. I shall inform the committee." More than likely Phoebe was already up there giving everyone their orders, Cecily thought as she smiled at Cranshaw.

"There is one more thing." He lifted his chin and looked

down his nose at her. "I assume that this was one of those rare occasions when you did not manage to get yourself entangled in police business. I appreciate your good sense and trust you will endeavor to restrain yourself in any future situations of this nature."

"Of course, Inspector," Cecily said loudly, hoping he didn't hear the faint strangled sound from Baxter.

Apparently he didn't, as he merely nodded, then left, followed by P.C. Northcott.

As the door closed behind them, Baxter let out his breath in an explosive snort. "That, madam, was an extremely close call."

Cecily grinned at him. "Our usual state of affairs when it comes to dealing with the good inspector, I'm afraid."

Baxter ran a nervous hand through his hair. "What is all this about Ian? I presume that is to whom you were referring when you talked about one of our staff deserting his wife."

Cecily's grin faded. "I was indeed. Such a tragic business. It seems that Ian was already married when he wed Gertie. His wife came looking for him and found him. It seems that she is pregnant, also. Ian returned to London with her as far as we know."

"Good Lord. Gertie with a child?"

"I know. It does take some getting used to, doesn't it?" She looked at him, wondering how he would take the next piece of news. "I've asked her to move back to the Pennyfoot. She can't manage in that cottage all alone. She can have the baby here and remain here for as long as she desires."

Baxter's eyebrows flickered, but he made no comment.

Cecily glanced at the clock on the mantelpiece and rose to her feet. "I must be on my way. There is so much to be done before the festivities tomorrow, and I want to have a word with Gertie before I leave."

She smiled wistfully at Baxter. "It would have been nice if Michael could have been home in time for May Day. It would have made a nice welcome for him."

"I am sure he will receive a warm welcome no matter when he arrives." Baxter opened the door as she approached him. "Now that your son is coming home, and with a new baby about the place, I am quite sure your time will be fully occupied. Perhaps that will prevent you from exposing yourself to danger in the future." He looked down at her as she reached him. "That will give me a great peace of mind," he added with a glint in his eye.

Standing close to him, Cecily met his gaze. "Piffle," she said softly. "You know very well that you would be bored beyond belief if you were no longer forced to watch over me."

To her intense interest, his expression altered. Once more his gaze left her breathless as he murmured, "If I may say so, madam, my life would be quite empty indeed if that were so. I sincerely hope and trust that you will always be in need of my presence, and of my protection."

So that was the thorn in his side every time she mentioned Michael, Cecily thought with a little rush of pleasure. He was afraid that she would no longer need him with her son at her side.

She tilted her head back to look at him and gave him a provocative smile. "Baxter," she said, looking deep into his eyes, "the Pennyfoot Hotel would be lost without you. And so, without a doubt, would I. Rest assured I shall always need you. Always."

She needed no words to know his response. The expression in his eyes was enough.